Quit Your Witchin'

AMY BOYLES

DEDICATION

This book is dedicated to all the working moms who feel frazzled to infinity most of the time and relish the five minutes a day they have to curl up with a good book before falling asleep.

ACKNOWLEDGMENTS

Thank you to my editor, Mary-Theresa Hussey for keeping this book on track.

ONE

Reid streaked toward me. "Ahh! It's going to hurt me!"

A crimson paper heart, cut from the best construction paper I could buy at Dollar General, soared toward my baby sister.

She shielded her face. "Stop it!"

"It's not going to hurt you," I said.

Reid clutched the burgundy curls that cascaded over her shoulders. "Then why is it chasing me?"

The heart flapped its body like wings, wobbling through the air. The thing wasn't exactly aerodynamic, though it was, in fact, aiming right toward Reid.

I cocked my head. She had a point. It might want to cut her.

My name is Dylan Apel and I'm a witch. My whole family is. Well, all of them except Reid, who was currently under attack from a decoration for the annual Silver Springs Valentine's Day dance. Yep, it was a community affair—come one, come all—from the geriatrics to the littlest ones. But this particular paper heart, limply beating its body around the room, was supposed to be hanging from the ceiling of the high school gymnasium, not magically bobbing around it.

Therein lay the problem.

My maternal grandmother, Hazel Horton, pushed up the sleeves of her sequined Valentine's sweater. The front had a naked cupid shooting an arrow. The back had the phrase, Will you be mine? She hadn't gotten a lot of offers on the latter yet.

Grandma grabbed me by the shoulders. "Dylan, you must wrangle them. Get control of the hearts before they shred our skin."

I stopped. "Me? Why me?"

My other sister, Seraphina—Sera for short—punched a heart to the floor and smashed it with her boot. "Because you're the one who caused this. They're supposed to be on the ceiling. Not attacking us."

That was indeed true. I might be a witch, but I'm not always great at magic. I'm getting better, but it takes a while to learn all the ins and outs of witchcraft. Apparently, right now was one of those out times.

"Grandma, what do I do?" I said.

She thrust a ball of twine in my hands. "Make a lasso. Corral them."

I stared from the twine to the flock of hearts flapping around the room. "Are you kidding?"

She clapped my shoulder. "Of course not. This is a battle. You must be in control. Take a stand. Here." She yanked the twine off the roll and secured it into a lasso. She snipped the end with a pair of scissors and shoved the string in my hands.

"Be one with the lasso, Dylan. Wrangle the hearts."

Reid caught the homicidal heart that had been chasing her. She ripped it in half. "Yeah, Dylan. Wrangle those hearts just like you did Roman's."

My little sister was talking about my boyfriend, Roman Bane, chief detective of Silver Springs, Alabama. "Yeah. Good thing he isn't here. He'd have a fit."

A side door swung open. "I've got the chairs."

I gnawed my lower lip. Speak of the devil.

Roman dropped the chairs and whipped off his black sunglasses. He stared at the mess of paper hearts flying about the room. Then Roman shot me a dark, scathing look.

"It was an accident?" I squeaked.

"Then why are you saying it like it's a question?"

"Because I don't know why?"

He sighed. Locked the door behind him and strode over. Roman was six foot two inches of chiseled muscle that made my knees jellify every time I plastered my gaze on him. He threaded his fingers through shoulder-length blond hair streaked white by the sun. His green eyes blazed as they searched the room. After several long moments his gaze settled on my family and me.

He nodded toward the string in my hand. "What's that?"

"A lasso?"

He tapped his fingers against slim hips. "You going to play cowboy?"

"I was thinking more along the lines of Wonder Woman."

He sidled over and smiled. The corners of his eyes crinkled, and his gaze filled with a goopy look that some might call love.

"I don't know why I try to be mad at you," he whispered.

"Because you can't stay that way," I said hopefully.

"Right." He exhaled. Planted a kiss on my forehead. "I brought you something."

A giggle of excitement bubbled in my throat. "What's that?"

He handed me a to-go cup of specialty coffee. "A mocha."

I took a quick sip. Warm java and chocolate mingled together over my tongue before sliding down my throat. "Oh, that's heaven." I glanced up at him and grinned. "You're the best."

His soft gaze settled on me. He thumbed my cheek and

smiled.

"Get a room, you two," Reid said. "We've got hearts to kill."

Roman coughed into his hand and straightened. He glanced around. "No one's seen this, have they?"

I placed the cup on a table and licked foam from my lip. "Nope."

"Let's keep it that way. I don't want the witch council crawling around this place."

So there were rules when it came to witchcraft. One of the main ones being no working magic in front of nonmagics, or regular folks. You know, your run-of-the-mill person. Normally, the penalty for working magic in front of people was death. Not just death. Being boiled alive.

Super ew. I know.

But luckily my family—well, me and Sera—were exempt from that punishment. We'd helped the community out by catching a killer a few months back, so now we were golden.

Sera pointed to the ceiling. "One of them's heading toward that open window. Dylan, Councilwoman Gladiolas will have a fit if she has to come down here and wipe a whole bunch of people's memories."

Okay, so I didn't want to push my luck on being golden.

Grandma threw her hands in the air. "If you two would just learn how to erase memories, then you wouldn't have to rely on someone else. You could do it yourselves."

I frowned. "Yeah, yeah. I've been busy. I'll learn it soon." That was true. I had been busy. I had a dress shop to run, magic to learn and be terrible at—you know all the hectic things that were part of life.

Roman grimaced. "I'm going to pretend like I'm not hearing any of this. Please don't tell me if you start wiping regular people's memories."

"That's not illegal," I said.

"The erasing isn't, but the part about working magic in front of them is."

I smiled. "Oh, well. I don't plan on that. Besides, I'm exempt from any punishment."

"I wouldn't push your privileges." Roman brushed his mouth over my ear. "Good luck. You know I love you."

I gulped down the egg in the back of my throat. Yes, I knew he loved me. He'd been telling me for a while now. Problem was, I couldn't quite tell him back. Don't shoot me, okay. Roman was hot. Roman was awesome. I know. I know. I'm a total loser for not being able to tell him.

It's just…love was heavy and stuff. I wasn't sure I was ready.

"Right back at you," I said. Total cop-out. I know.

Roman's jaw clenched as he smiled.

A zinger of pain shot into my heart. I felt like it crushed him a little every time I didn't say "I love you." As bad as it made me feel to witness his hurt, I wasn't going to voice something I wasn't ready to embrace.

"All right, Grandma," I said. "Show me how to work this thing."

She gave me the quick and dirty, which I can sum up as, and I quote, "Be one with the lasso. Aim it at your target and throw."

Seriously. That's all the instruction I got.

So I aimed and threw. At every single heart. And there were like, one hundred of them. But I managed to get them all, including the one threatening to flap right out the window.

"Whew." I smeared a line of sweat off my forehead. "Glad that's over. Someone remind me never to try getting decorations to hang themselves again."

Sera smoothed down her glossy chocolate-colored locks.

"Don't worry. After fighting paper hearts, I'm pretty sure we're all in agreement on that."

"Yeah," Reid whined. "You almost got me all wounded and stuff."

I rolled my eyes. "Did you get even one paper cut?"

Reid inspected her arm. "I thought I had one."

"Well until you find that one, I'm going with no."

She stuck her tongue out at me.

"I'd hate for your tongue to freeze that way. What would Rick think?"

A sappy look smudged Reid's face. "Isn't he dreamy?"

Rick Beck was Reid's boyfriend and our next-door neighbor. Reid had drooled over him for a good year or so before they finally started dating.

Sera sighed dramatically. "Yeah. He's dreamier than dreamy. In fact, I think he's the dreamiest."

Reid scoffed. "Whatever."

Roman tapped his foot. "All this teenage arguing is hard to rip away from, but I'm going to grab the chairs."

I squeezed his marble-hard bicep. "Thanks."

"You got it."

Reid pointed. "You missed a heart, Dylan."

I followed her finger until I saw it. One lone heart flapped desperately against the bleachers.

My family stared at it. No one moved to grab it.

"Don't rush over, everyone," I said. "I'll go save the day."

"Thank goodness," Sera said. "You're our hero, Dylan."

I grumbled something not appropriate under my breath and made my way to the heart. It beat sadly against the aluminum seating. I figured I could catch it with my hands. There was no need for my magic lasso, though I might keep that thing nearby. See if I could spell it to make people tell the truth.

You know, pretend I really was Wonder Woman. Because that's what all sane twenty-eight-year-old women with their own dressmaking businesses did. They dressed up and pretended they were comic book characters.

Almost sounded normal.

I snatched the paper heart and folded it in half. It fought but settled down once I had it secured.

As I turned back toward my family, I noticed something glinting in the bleachers. I peered through the slats and saw a watch. As I looked closer, I noticed the watch was attached to a hand, and the hand, an arm. My gaze slid on up. A man was stuffed between the slats. His head lopped over at a sick angle. You didn't have to be a coroner to know there wasn't any breath left in those lungs.

I stumbled backward. "Roman, I think you need to get over here."

He chuckled. "The heart giving you a hard time?"

"No. It's worse," I croaked.

He crossed over. "What is it?"

I glanced back at him. "A dead body."

TWO

"Who do you think it was?" Sera asked a couple of hours later.

We sat in my dress shop, Perfect Fit, drinking mugs of hot chocolate that Sera had brought over from her bakery next door. Sera's shop may have been called Sinless Confections, but there was absolutely nothing sinless about her goods. One bite of her baked treats and you felt deliciously sinful—in a good way.

I fingered a dollop of whip cream into my mouth. "No clue. I'd never seen him before."

Sera glanced out the window onto Main Street. Antique stores, a baby boutique and a barber shop stared back at us. Our quaint hamlet still managed to have a thriving downtown, which was super awesome, if you asked me. In fact, a shop was opening across the street.

"Have you met that new owner yet?" she asked.

I smacked my lips. "No. Dying to. I don't even know what sort of store's going in."

Sera nodded. "Well, it looks like she's coming over."

I set my cup down as the bell above the door tinkled.

A cold wind whipped through the store. I shivered as a five-foot-ten supermodel of a woman with legs up to her eyeballs sauntered in. Chestnut hair hung in loose movie-star curls around her face and over her shoulders. She wore black shiny boots, tight jeans, a slim wool coat and enough makeup for the entire town.

My mouth dried at the very sight of her.

She beamed a broad smile of perfect teeth. "Whew, is it totally cold out there or what?" She stomped imaginary snow off her boots. "It's so cozy in here I might just melt away."

"Well come on in, get yourself warmed up," I said cheerfully.

"Thank you so much. Mmm hmm. My momma always said I don't have enough skin on these bones to keep me warm."

She tugged the wool cap off her head and shook out her hair. "Anyway, I'm totally opening up the store right across the street. I'm so excited about it I could just squeal with pleasure. But anyway, I'll spare y'all that." She stuck out a hand. "I'm Dewy Dewberry."

Sera and I shook her hand and gave her our names.

Dewy shrugged off the cold. As she spoke she gestured up, down, and sideways with her arms while her eyes opened wide. She looked like a deer in headlights. Like a constant deer in headlights. "Oh, I totally know all about y'all. Everyone knows the Apel sisters. Mmm hmmm."

I shot a concerned look at Sera. "Everyone knows about us?"

A twinkle sparkled in Dewy's eyes. She leaned in real close and whispered, "You know how it is with us witches. Can't keep our mouths shut." She straightened to full Amazonian height. "All I can say is y'all are absolutely legendary, the way you've put bad witches behind bars. I'm totally in awe."

I lifted my eyebrows sharply. "You're a witch?"

"Mmm hmm," Dewy said.

Here's the thing about witches—whenever they appear in my life, bad things happen—like people try to kill me.

She tugged off her coat and threw it onto a chair. Underneath, she wore a tight red sweater that showcased a boob job and tiny waist.

It was a good boob job. I had to say.

I squirmed, suddenly feeling incredibly inadequate. A freakin' Barbie doll was standing in my shop and in comparison I felt like Raggedy Ann. Or maybe Holly Hobby wearing her quilted dress and calico bonnet.

Dewy grinned. "Of course I'm a witch. We witches have to stick together. Mmm hmm." Her gaze slewed to one side of the room. "So that's why I'm here. So we can bond. Mmm hmm."

Who was she, like the guy from Sling Blade who said Mmm hmm at the end of every sentence?

Try not to judge, Dylan. Be good.

Sera gave Dewy a sweet smile. "Well, we're glad to have you in Silver Springs. We always love it when a new shop opens downtown. We'd rather see 'em open than close. Isn't that right, Dylan?"

I was staring at Dewy's boobs. They kinda mesmerized me.

"Right, Dylan?" Sera poked me.

I jumped. "Huh? Oh, yeah. We love new businesses." I sighed. That was true. To be honest, if it came right down to it, I'd rather a witch open a store in Silver Springs than see an empty shop.

What can I say? I cared about the economy of my little town.

I forced a smile. "We're glad to have you here." Witch or no witch, I guessed. "Please, sit. Tell us about yourself."

Dewy flashed another smiled. She sat like a perfect lady, crossed one shiny boot atop the other and laced her hands over one knee.

"I've totally come to bring my particular talents to Silver Springs."

Sera quirked an interested brow. "This town needs all the talent it can get."

I nodded. "Absolutely. We've had the same shops for a few years now. If your store brings more happiness to the residents here, that's great."

Me personally, I design clothes that make people feel fabulous. As I've already explained, Sera's baked goods do something similar. Eating one of her cookies is like getting a hug of warmth and goodness. Seriously. You feel like a better person after finishing it.

"So what do you do?" Sera said. "What's your witchy power?"

Dewy nibbled her bottom lip for a second. "My talent's just like yours, Dylan. I make clothes. And from what people say, my clothes make them feel wrapped up in satin."

My heart stopped beating. Was she supposed to be competition? That wasn't good. I didn't want another dressmaker in town.

Let alone one who was a witch.

"You know." Dewy giggled. "I've heard interesting rumors about y'all. How you've worked magic in front of regular people without getting in trouble with the council. It's pretty interesting stuff. Mmm hmm."

I nodded. "Yeah."

Dewy flipped a curl from her eyes. "We all know the penalty for working magic in front of nonmagics—death."

I clicked my tongue, trying to ignore the creepy vibe I was getting from this witch. "Yeah, well. We slipped up a couple of times—once when I was teaching Sera how to bake using her magic. The pots and pans floated out into the street and half the town had to have their memories erased. But it was an accident."

"Besides," Sera added. "We were brand-new witches. That's one reason why Councilwoman Gladiolas didn't punish us."

I snapped my fingers. "That's right. The law states that you have to be working magic in front of regular people on purpose. We never did that." I laughed nervously. "We're just plain old morons."

Dewy smiled tightly but said nothing.

Across the street, Roman's black SUV rolled to a stop. He killed the engine and slipped out.

All gazes shifted to the window.

"Who is that?" Dewy cooed.

Roman waited for a car to pass; then he crossed the tarmac. With his long strides, it only took an instant for him to reach the shop. He opened the door and slid his sunglasses to the top of his head.

"Hey," he said in that husky voice of his. The one that made my bones fizzle.

"Hey." The three of us replied in unison.

His gaze settled on me. My breath hitched as his green eyes barbed my heart to my spinal cord.

Dewy fanned herself. "Oh my gosh, I totally thought a Greek god just entered the building. You're not a god, are you?"

His eyes stayed glued on me. "Not last I checked."

"Thank goodness, because I'd need to go home and change into something more appropriate." Dewy rose and extended her hand. Roman slid his gaze from me to her. "Dewy Dewberry. I'm opening the shop across the street." She slinked forward, brushing the top half of her body against him. "Oh my gosh, I'm so sorry. Did my breast touch you? That pesky thing. Has a mind of its own. In fact, the other one does, too. Sometimes they just can't help themselves."

Roman stepped away from her projectile boobs. "Roman Bane," he said curtly. "I work for the police department."

Her ruby lips split into a smile. "So I call you when I need protection."

"Roman's busy protecting my family," I nearly shouted. "There's lots of other guys, though. There's Steve Howie. He's nice. Writes a lot of speeding tickets. Yep. Plenty of men on the force who'd be happy to help out if you get scared by a possum or something. In fact, last I heard we were having a hard time with hoboes hanging around Main. Isn't that right, Sera? Didn't I hear something about hoboes?"

Everyone in the room stared at me openmouthed. You could have heard a feather drop.

I nudged Sera. "Hoboes?"

Sera was such a great sister. She kept her face masked as she said, "Yes, I heard we've had some hobo problems. Be sure to lock your door."

Roman rolled his eyes.

"Did you identify the body?" I asked.

He shook his head. "Not yet. But we're working on it."

Dewy grabbed Roman's arm. "A body? What happened?"

"We found an unidentified person earlier today."

Dewy slipped her hips toward Roman's, shoving her other breast into his rib cage. "Do you think I should be worried?"

Roman peeled her off him and said, "There's nothing for anyone to worry about."

She grabbed him again. "But if there is?"

His face crimsoned. Roman unhooked her claw and said, "We'll let the public know first thing. Trust me."

She gave him a seductive smile. "Oh, I do. I can already tell that you're someone I can trust with my body." Dewy shook her head. "I mean my life."

I stopped myself from punching her in the face.

Roman glanced at me. "I wanted to make sure you're all right."

I shrugged. "I'm fine. Don't worry about me."

He jiggled the car keys in his hand. "I need to go check on Boo. I'll catch up with you later."

"How is he?" I asked.

"Hanging in there."

Boo was Richard Bane, Roman's father. We'd found him a couple months ago in the forest behind Castle Witch. Before he surfaced, he'd been missing for nearly twenty years. When we discovered Boo he looked like a wild man, wearing little more than buckskin. He remembered who he was, but not much more than that.

And he insisted we call him Boo.

Don't ask me. I couldn't figure it out. Neither could Roman, but we went along with it.

Roman left and Dewy licked her lips. "Boy, is he some hot stuff. Mmm hmm. I mean totally super hot. Girls, I may need some ice to chill down my girlie parts."

Um. Okay.

Sera cleared her throat. "He sure is. And he's all Dylan's."

Dewy's mouth curved into a smirk. Though the smirk looked sarcastic, those wide eyes made Barbie look totally ditsy. "Oh my gosh. Wow. All yours, huh?"

An uncomfortable giggle bubbled from my mouth. "Yeah. All mine."

She looked me up and down like royalty sizing up a peasant. "He must be crazy about you, then. Must totally be in love with you. He is, right? In love with you? I mean, I couldn't tell— what with my breasts getting all in the way and everything—but he is, isn't he?"

I cleared my throat. "He's said it a time or two."

"Gosh, a guy like that, you must be doing all you can to hang onto him. Mmm hmm. Lots of women would throw themselves at a man that good-looking."

You don't say.

Dewy swiped a finger over the rim of her lips. "I'd totally make sure he knew I loved him. Mmm hmm."

"Telling a guy you love him doesn't give you any security," Sera said.

Dewy tapped a finger to her lips. "This Roman's different. He likes to be told he's loved. I can tell."

My jaw fell to the floor. Before I had a chance to compose myself and think of some sort of coherent reply, the door swung open.

Jenny Butts entered. She pumped her hands as she greeted us. "Y'all. Y'all. Y'all. There's a new store opening. Have y'all seen it?"

"Pretty sure we just did," Sera said drily.

Dewy waved an immaculately manicured hand. "Hey, Jenny."

Jenny fluffed her blonde Marilyn Monroe Curls. "Dewy! So good to see you. I didn't realize you knew the Apels."

"We just met," I snapped.

"We sure did," Dewy said. "And I know I'm going to love my new neighbors. We're gonna be just like sisters."

"Sure," I said. If you wanted to throw your sister off a cliff.

"In fact, we were getting all sisterly a minute ago. I was telling Dylan how I would be all over my hunky boyfriend, making sure he knew I loved him. That was, if I had a super-hot boyfriend like that Roman of hers."

Jenny grabbed her throat as a ball of laughter tumbled from her lips. "Dylan? Tell a guy she loves him? I'd love to see that.

Dylan might have a boyfriend, but she swore off men years ago."

"That's not true, Jenny," I said.

"In fact, she hasn't dated anyone since Colten Blacklock broke her heart in high school."

"I'm standing right here, you know," I said.

Jenny scoffed. "It's not like this is private information. Everyone knows that about you and Colten."

"They do now," I said.

Jenny shot me an ultra-fake smile. "Anyway, I'm glad to see that you met the Apels, Dewy. Want to go have some lunch?"

Dewy brightened at that. "Lunch sounds fantastic. I've worked up a real appetite getting to know the folks in town."

Jenny cinched her coat. "Great. You can ride with me. I'm parked out front."

Dewy rose and shrugged her coat back on. "I'll catch up with you in a sec."

Jenny gave a wiggly wave and left.

Good riddance.

Dewy threaded her fingers through her sexy curls. She flashed me that wide-eyed doe look of hers. "I think you asked about my witch power. Is that right? Didn't you ask?"

Sera clicked her tongue. "You're absolutely right."

"Not sure I want to know," I whispered under my breath.

Sera shot me a look of death. I smiled sweetly at her.

Dewy dug the heel of her boot into the floor. "I design clothes. You know that already. Mmm hmm." She pursed her lips. "But there's totally like one thing that separates my clothes from yours."

I raised an eyebrow. "And what's that?"

Dewy swung open the front door. "Well. Yeah. Um hmm. So you see, my clothes do this one teensy weensy thing. I can't help it, but they do. They kind of seduce people."

"Oookayy," I said. "What exactly does that mean?"

Her lips coiled into a devilish grin. "Well, uh-huh. Yeah. That means I can totally seduce whoever I want. All I have to do is wrap them up in something I made."

She gave an innocent finger wave and said, "Toodles." The door slammed shut as she left.

I turned to Sera. "I have a weird feeling about her."

"I've got the same one," Sera said.

"So you're thinking what I'm thinking?"

Her blue eyes darkened. "Yep. Dewy Dewberry wants one thing."

I grimaced. "And that is?"

"To seduce your boyfriend."

THREE

We had a big family supper planned for that night. Roman wanted to get Boo interacting with more people, and I enjoyed food, so it seemed like a good idea. We didn't have large dinners too often, so getting folks together was always nice—especially when it was near romantic holidays and involved boyfriends.

"Reid, would you please stop hogging the hairbrush?" Sera said.

Reid had been standing in the bathroom for fifteen minutes. She'd run the brush through her hair for most of that time, I was pretty sure.

"I need to make my locks shine," Reid whined.

"Then put some styling serum on them," Sera snapped. "It's my turn. Brock will be here any minute."

Reid rolled her eyes. "Great. The monkey king arrives. Is he bringing his monkey entourage?"

Sera sniffed. "I don't know. I doubt it. And what's with you acting like a little girl? My boyfriend is king of the winged monkeys. Yours is just a regular guy."

That was true. All of it. Sera had met Brock Odom a couple of months ago. The moment they laid eyes on each other it was instant love. I know. I was there.

On the other hand Rick Beck's claim to fame was that he looked awesome shirtless. I also know this because that's how he mowed his lawn in the spring and the summer and the fall. Sans shirt. The view, if I do say so myself, was spectacular.

Hey, both guys had their perks if you asked me.

The doorbell rang. Sera scowled at Reid. "That better not be Brock. I need at least five more minutes."

I patted her shoulder. "If it's him, I'll offer some monkey juice to keep him occupied."

"Very funny. Monkey juice doesn't exist."

"I know. It was a joke."

I bounded through the craftsman cottage we shared with my grandmother and her bodyguard, Nan. The dining room table was set, and the whole house smelled like country cooking—cornbread, fried okra, turnip greens—you name it, we had it bubbling either on the stove or in the oven.

Grandma popped in from the kitchen with a World War II helmet on.

"Worried that the food is going to attack?" I asked.

"No. Worried I need it for whoever's at the door."

I hooked both hands beneath the lip of the helmet and gently tugged it off. "It's only the guests we invited. Remember? I don't think anyone's arriving who wants to start another witch war."

She fluffed the ends of her triangle-shaped head of hair. "You never know, Dylan. It pays to be prepared."

"Let's answer the door and see who it is. If it's someone dangerous, I'll return the hat."

Grandma nodded in agreement.

When I opened the door, the entire guest list stood on the other side as if they'd carpooled together.

Brock Odom, monkey king extraordinaire, wore a black motorcycle jacket and jeans. Dark hair brushed his shoulders. He tapped a finger to his forehead. "Hey, Dylan. Good to see y'all," he said in that buttery voice of his. I swear, the sound sent tingles up my spine. There was no telling what it did to Sera.

Rick Beck stood behind him. A smile beamed from his crystal-blue eyes. His brown hair was short. Muscles rippled through his tight sweater. "Evening, ladies. Thanks for inviting me to dinner."

"Thanks for coming," I said. "Come on in."

Rick held up a cell phone. "Reid left this in my car."

My sisters thundered through the house and into the room.

"Did you find my cell phone?" Reid asked breathlessly.

"Right were you left it. On the floorboard of my car."

Reid flashed him a huge smile. "Thank you."

Rick would be well taken care of by Reid, and Sera would snatch up Brock in about two seconds.

Grandma worried the rope of pearls wrapped around her neck. "Roman, it's good to see you. Boo, I'm so glad you decided to have dinner with us."

Boo Bane wore his silver hair long. Pictures of him from his youth showed a man with short hair. But something about the wild had changed him. He wore long locks and a beard he refused to shave. For as scraggly as he looked, the man was all kitten.

Boo took Grandma's hands. "Thank you for having me. Have I been here before?"

Oh yeah, Boo didn't remember much from his past.

Grandma squinted. "Not that I recall."

Boo swept by us, leaving Roman and me alone. Roman entwined his hand in mine. "You look beautiful."

He nuzzled the top of my head. A moan edged up the back of my throat. "I look the same as when you saw me earlier." Minus the fake boobs, meaning Dewy Dewberry.

"No. You look better. Smell better."

"The wonders of soap and water."

He inhaled. "Keep doing it."

I pulled him to the side so that we stood in front of the antique cherry buffet. "I wanted to give you your Valentine's present."

A serious expression crossed his angular face. "That seems suspicious."

My heart pounded with worry. "What? Why?"

Roman threw me a look of mock concern. "Giving me my present early? It must be something horrible. If I hate it, you have time to buy me another one. A better one."

I poked his ribs. "It's not horrible."

He flinched, a chuckle escaping his lips. "Must be worse than horrible. What's worse than horrible?"

"You're worse than horrible."

Roman clutched his heart. "You can't mean it."

I giggled. Roman gave me a thousand-watt smile, and my muscle control melted. I inhaled his musky scent and opened one of the drawers. I handed him a slim, rectangular box.

He glanced down. "You didn't have to get me anything."

"Now there's the response I was looking for."

He slid a sinewy hand over the crimson bow. "I don't have your gift with me."

"You don't have to get me anything."

He glanced at the gold heart sitting at the bottom of my throat. "Right. I'm going to have to work hard to show up your Christmas gift."

I fingered the delicate heart with the single diamond resting in its stem. "This was a great Christmas present. Best one I ever got."

He glanced at the box. Dark smudgy lashes framed his gorgeous green eyes. "Maybe I should open this on Valentine's."

"No," I nearly shrieked. "Would you stop being so difficult and just open it?"

"As you wish." He lifted the lid, revealing a royal-blue silk tie.

I fisted my hands and pressed them against my cheeks. "Do you like it?"

A slow smile curled on his lips. "You made this?"

I nodded nervously.

He lifted the tie from the box and ran his fingers over the silky surface. "It's going to match the dress you're wearing to the dance," he said, realizing its purpose.

I nodded again.

He wrapped it around his neck and proceeded to create a perfect tie.

"What are you doing?"

"I'm wearing it."

"Now?"

He nodded. "Now. I love it so much I don't want to put it back in the box. Besides," he said, glancing at his reflection in the mirror hanging over the buffet, "it feels good. I feel good. I love it."

I scoffed. "You're just saying that."

He turned and entwined his fingers in mine. "It's the best Valentine's gift I've ever got. Hands down."

The urge to have a serious public display of affection tugged at me. So instead of embarrassing myself, I straightened the expression on my face and said, "Don't spill anything on it. I'm not cleaning it for you."

"You don't look like a maid to me."

I encircled my hand over his arm. "Come on. Let's go get some dinner."

Grandma had made rib-sticking food—with Sera's help, of course. The of course part of that was Southern cornbread dressing with chicken. Delicious. I'd just plopped a scoop down on my plate when the bell rang again.

My eyes met Sera's. "Are we missing someone?"

"I don't think so."

I scooted back my chair and crossed to the door. I opened it to find my paternal grandmother, Milly Jones, on the other side. She wore a puffy coat zipped up to her chin and a wool hat yanked down to her eyes. Her usual shoulder decoration of Polly Parrot, however, was absent. Instead a boa constrictor was wrapped around her neck like a scarf. It had scales the color of bone with pale yellow markings. Its tongue shot out as it tasted the air. My stomach queased.

Milly stroked its head. "I heard there was a dinner going on over here, so I thought I'd join the fun."

"Um. That thing's not going to eat me, is it?"

"Nah. It's not hungry. Just ate a rat."

Sera popped up beside me. "Ah!" She shuddered. Then she slicked back her hair, regaining her composure. "Where's Polly?"

Milly shrugged. "I'm giving him a break."

"By torturing him with a snake?"

Milly frowned. "Listen, toots, we've all got to do things that make us uncomfortable from time to time. It's good for Polly. Puts some hair on his chest."

"He's made of wood," I said.

"Exactly."

Well, I could see this conversation wasn't going anywhere.

I swept the air with my hand. "Come on in. We'd be glad to add one more." I brought my finger to my lips. "But no talk about you-know-what. Reid's boyfriend is here."

"What?" Milly said.

"Ix-nay on the agic-may."

She squinted. "What?"

"Magic," I hissed. "No talking about it."

Milly nodded. "You won't get one peep out of me."

Sera scratched her ear. "Sure."

Milly sat in the extra chair I found for her. "So what's this I hear about a body being found in the gym, Roman? We got a serial killer on the loose?"

Roman coughed into his napkin. "Hardly. No ID on the victim, but he happened to have a picture of himself in his wallet."

"Like a snapshot?" I asked.

"No, more like a wallet-sized studio pic."

I quirked an eyebrow. "Was there anyone else in it?"

Roman forked a glob of dressing. "Nope." He popped it in his mouth and pulled a wallet from his back pocket. "Here it is."

I stared at the image. A middle-aged man with brown hair and a bushy mustache sat in front of a background that looked like a high school picture twenty years too late, replete with a soft gray backdrop and laser beams.

I was surprised the guy wasn't holding his pet cat. "He has kind eyes."

"Let me see," Reid said, snatching the pic. "I've never heard of anyone having kind eyes."

Rick peered over her shoulder. "If you ask me, he looks smug. Like he's asking for someone to punch him in the face."

We all stared at Rick, waiting for the joke.

Reid rubbed his arm. "Oh Rick, you're such a kidder."

Rick said nothing.

"He looks familiar," Boo said.

Now the conversation really died.

"What?" Roman said.

Boo nodded. "He does. Looks familiar."

Milly met my gaze. "Tell us how, Boo."

"Well, let me see." He pinched the picture between two fingers and studied it. "Seems to me there's something about those eyes. Like Dylan said, they're kind."

Roman scrubbed a hand down face. "Is that all? Just the eyes?"

"No. There's something else, too. Can't put a finger on it, but I guarantee that man's a wizard."

You could have heard a spec of sawdust fall through the air. All eyes widened. Milly dismissed it with a wave. "Oh well, cat's out of the bag now."

Rick perked up. "You mean that guy plays Dungeons & Dragons with all the other losers on Saturdays at the library? Is that how he's a wizard?"

"Yep," I said quickly. "Exactly."

"Are you sure?" Roman asked Boo.

Boo's gaze flickered back to the picture. He stroked his whiskers and said, "Pretty sure." He glanced at Milly. "Would you care to enlighten us as to why you have a boa constrictor around your neck?"

"To liven things up. Keep people in line. Not to mention, personal protection. You never know when you might need a snake."

"I take it he's magic."

I slapped a palm to my forehead.

Milly shrugged. "Don't worry about it, toots. As soon as I

arrived, I knew we'd be doing some memory erasing."

"But we're trying to be good. I'm trying to be good."

She ripped open a roll and slathered a pat of butter on it. "Then close your ears. No big deal. Besides, it'll give me time to teach you the correct way to do the spell."

Grandma Hazel fluffed her hair. "That's exactly what they need, Milly. Correct instruction." She flashed me a triumphant grin. "Now you don't have an excuse not to learn it."

"Great," I mumbled.

Milly wiped her mouth with a napkin. "Since that's decided, let's get to the juicy stuff. I heard there's a new witch in town."

Rick whistled. "I don't know about a witch, but there's sure some hot new store owner."

"Bro, not the way to talk in front of your lady," Brock chastised.

"And you like this guy?" I added to Reid.

She sniffled. "He's only joking. Right, Rick? You're only joking."

Rick smacked his lips. "Of course. I didn't notice any new folks in town. Especially not a tall, leggy one who dresses like a stripper."

Grandma fluffed her hair. "Well, I did. Saw her putting up her sign. She's opening a clothing shop right across the street from Dylan." Grandma reached over and patted my hand. "Dear, I hope she isn't competition for you, because in the looks department you don't stand a chance."

"Thanks, Grandma. As a matter of fact, as Milly said, she's going to be direct competition."

"Oh? What's her power?" Grandma said.

I glanced at Rick, who was way into the conversation. I didn't want to talk too much about witches, but like Milly said, his memory was going to have to be wiped anyway, so who cared?

"Claims she can seduce folks with her clothes."

"She can seduce me anytime," Rick said.

"Really?" I said to Reid. "You still want to date him?"

"He's not normally like this," she whimpered.

Grandma tsked. "Not a good power to have. At the outset it might seem all well and wonderful. But it's dangerous. Reminds me of the time the fairies wanted to give me some pixie dust. Told me it would make me fly. But you know what?"

"What?" Sera asked.

Grandma jabbed the air with her finger. "It didn't work because I wasn't a fairy."

I nodded. "And the point is?"

"Some people will buy the clothes thinking they're love potions," Milly snarled. "A girl buys an outfit and wears it for her boyfriend, hoping he'll propose. What happens is that the boy falls a little in love with the girl, but he also falls in love with the witch who made it."

"Not good," I said. Mental note. Do not buy any of Dewy's clothes.

"What's the witch's name?" Milly asked.

"Dewy Dewberry," I said.

She arched a brow. "I know that name."

"You do?"

Milly nodded.

"Is she in the witch registry?" Sera said. There was an official Registry of Witches. I'd never seen the thing, but my sisters and I knew of its existence.

Milly gnawed on a roll. "No, she's not on the official registry."

"She's not?" I said.

"No. Only good witches are on that."

I frowned. "Then how do you know her name?"

"Because there's an unofficial registry."

Sera arched an eyebrow. "An unofficial registry? Why didn't you tell us about this before?"

"Because it's classified. Not everyone knows about it," Milly said.

Slowly, realization dawned on me. "And let me guess—that unofficial registry holds all the bad witches."

Milly picked a piece of food from her teeth. "That's right. So guess how I know Dewy's name?"

I gasped. "Because she's on the unofficial registry."

Milly winked. "You got it, toots."

FOUR

"Tell me about Dewy Dewberry," I said to Milly.

Sera, Reid and I stood on her front porch. A wind blasted across, tinkling her wooden wind chimes. I wrapped my arms tight over my chest.

"What do you want to know?" Milly said.

I pushed past her. "Everything."

"We don't have a lot of time," Sera said. "I put the BE RIGHT BACK sign up on my door, which gives me about ten minutes, tops."

When I stepped inside Milly's old two-story home, the first thing I noticed was Polly Parrot. He screeched and flew over, perching on my shoulder. I tickled his chin.

"He's wood, you know," Reid said.

"I know that. But he might like to be petted," I said. "Where's that terrible snake of yours?"

Milly caned across the room. "He's in the bathroom. Polly keeps trying to peck his eyes out."

"Self-preservation," I said. "Can't blame him there."

Milly lowered herself onto a chair and splayed her legs on either side of her cane. She wore stereotypical old-woman clothing of a bland knee-length skirt, support hose, and black square orthopedic shoes.

Milly scowled. "You want to look at the unofficial registry."

Sera yanked off her gloves. "We only want to know the dirt on Dewy."

Milly glared at us. "Why?"

"Because I think she wants to steal my boyfriend." I sighed, rubbing the worry lines from my forehead.

Milly cackled. What a sensitive grandmother I had. "What makes you say that?"

I crossed my arms. "Oh, I don't know. Maybe the fact that she brushed her boobs up against him and then later told me she could seduce anyone, might have had something to do with it. Plus she was super creepy, asking questions about how we've worked magic in front of regular people and not been punished for it."

Milly tipped her head from side to side. "So you want the dirt on her, eh?"

"As much as you've got."

She rose and caned over to a bookshelf. I scanned the titles. They looked completely normal. Cookbooks, some Mark Twain, a few romance novels. Nothing out of the ordinary. Though I had to say, of all the people I knew, Milly seemed the least likely to be interested in a little bit of romance.

But I'd been known to be wrong before.

She washed a hand over the case. A shimmering wave buoyed outward. The bookshelves transformed from their bright and cheery colors to dark hues, thick casings and wide bindings.

"What?" Sera said.

"You didn't think I actually read that stuff, did you?"

Sera flicked a streak of hair from her face. "I don't know.

Maybe."

"Ha! Had you fooled."

"They didn't fool me," Reid chirped. "Not a bit. I knew it was a fake."

I rolled my eyes. "No you didn't."

Milly pointed to a thick black tome. "One of you grab that."

I hoisted the book from the case. It weighed close to five pounds. Scallop-edged yellow paper protruded from the side. I laid it on the table with a huff. Gilded script with curled letters read Registry of Witches.

We all crouched around.

Milly rested her cane on a chair. She spread her fingers over the book and said, "Open sesame."

I quirked a brow.

"Best password on the planet. No one ever expects it," she said.

The book tore open, and pages flipped as if a wind were blowing it. Glittering magical dust fluttered up into the air. My sisters and I took a collective step backward.

"What do you want to see, Milly Jones?"

The book talked! I glanced around to make sure no one else had entered the room. That in fact the book had spoken. Yep, it was only the four of us. The ancient tome—or recent tome, or book, or whatever—had a voice and used it.

In fact, it kinda sounded like James Earl Jones.

"I need to know about the doings of a particular witch."

"And which witch would that be?" the voice boomed.

Seriously, it was like having Darth Vader in the house. A chill raced down my spine.

"You old jokester," Milly said.

The book laughed. "Like my alliteration?"

Milly thumbed her nose. "Which witch would that be? Book,

you got me there!"

"Please, call me Reggie."

"Reggie?" Sera said.

Reggie swiveled toward Sera. "Who is this?"

"My granddaughter, Sera."

"Nice to meet you," it said. "Yes, the name Reggie is a nickname for the Registry of Witches."

"But we're not even looking for the official registry," Reid said.

"And who is this?" Reggie said.

Milly introduced them.

"What is it you seek, Milly Jones?" Reggie asked.

Milly laid her palms flat on the open book and said, "I need to see the other side. The dark side of the light. The place where there is mystery and past, the place where the others rest."

Reggie swirled round and round, creating a tornado of sparkling magic above it. My hair lifted, and I edged back, hoping the thing didn't explode in my face.

Pages rippled and turned until the book was at its last page—a blank one. Then dark block letters appeared—Unofficial Registry of Witches.

"Whoa," Reid said. "This is serious stuff."

"How does it work?" Sera whispered to Milly. "Is this the real book or what?"

Reggie shivered. "I am a copy of the official registry. The original sits in a secret place and is guarded by the council of witches. When something is added or deleted from that book, the information eventually trickles to me and my brothers. Since it was declared that only good witches could exist in that book, the unofficial registry was created."

"For bad witches," Milly said.

"Why not just add bad doings in the official registry?" Sera asked.

Milly snorted. "Because the witch council doesn't like to think that their own kind do bad things—and when witches do turn bad, the masses don't need to know about it. At least that was their thought process. But with the rise of magic stealing, all that changed. Bad deeds needed to be known because the deeds themselves were, at times, hideous. That's why your father created the unofficial registry."

Sera's voice trembled. "Our father?"

Milly nodded. "Your father created it in the hopes that it would help others. He died before it was presented to the council."

Reggie cleared his throat. "But his work lives on. Before he passed over, Jeffrey Apel created a spell that updates me automatically. When a witch does a bad deed, it ends up in here."

"How many copies of you are there? The official registry, I mean?" Sera asked.

"A few. Most of them are in important places, like at the witch police headquarters, but some are with individuals at secret locations. In case something destroyed all the known copies, there would still be backups."

Milly cleared her throat. "Does that answer all the pansy-bottomed questions? 'Cause we need to get on with this."

No one said anything.

Milly stared at Reggie. "I need to know about one Dewy Dewberry. What event put her on the bad registry?"

"Let me see," Reggie said. Pages flipped to the right. It stopped. The pages flipped back left. "Ahh. Here she is."

A picture of Dewy appeared on the thick vellum. Her hair was a little shorter and her boobs weren't as big, but it was the same witch.

Reggie cleared his throat. Or binding. Or whatever. "It's hard to say if Dewy was ever really on the straight and narrow. She always got in trouble at school. Minor things like setting a pile of leaves on fire or even locking a teacher out of the classroom. Events that could have ironed themselves out had Miss Dewberry allowed them to."

"But they didn't," Milly said.

"No. Five years ago Miss Dewberry was caught in Fairyland trying to steal a unicorn."

"A unicorn?" I said.

The book pivoted toward me. Its pages pulsed as if breathing. "Who's this?"

"My granddaughter, Dylan."

"Pleased to make your acquaintance, Your Majesty."

I took it that Reggie was referring to my short stint as Queen Witch of the South. I shook my head. "I'm not queen anymore. Now, I'm just Dylan."

"As you say, Just Dylan."

"No, you don't have to put anything in front of my name. It's just Dylan. Not queen."

"Yes, Just Dylan. I understand."

No, you don't. But whatever.

Sera leaned forward. "So Dewy was caught trying to steal a unicorn? Who on earth would try that?"

"It wasn't any unicorn Miss Dewberry was trying to steal. It was a baby unicorn."

I knitted my brows together. "A baby? Why would she take one of them?"

Milly drummed her fingers on the table. "Babies are known to be more powerful than adults in the first year or two of their lives. Their magic is strong."

A wave of dread spread over my body. "So do you think she

wanted to skin the baby for its power?"

"Or take its horn. Reggie?" Milly said.

"No one knows. Miss Dewberry never admitted to the why of her crime. Luckily she was caught outside Fairyland. The unicorn was safely returned to its parents."

"So that put her on the bad registry," I said.

"It did, Just Dylan. She served three years in witch prison and was released. Her whereabouts are currently unknown."

"Oh they're known all right," Reid said. "She's here in Silver Springs."

The edges of Reggie's cover curled up. "She is?"

"Sure is," Reid said.

"Mmm. Do you perchance get to see her on a regular basis?"

I sighed. "She works across the street from us."

His pages flipped from side to side. "Might I come with you so that I may keep abreast of her activities?"

I cocked a brow in Milly's direction. "Do you think it should come with us?"

"Sure. Reggie may be able to give you more information. He knows how to get back here when he needs to."

"He does?" Reid said.

Milly smirked. "He's magical, toots. One day you may know what that is. But until then, you'll remain powerless."

Reid's expression crumpled. "Thanks for reminding me."

We said our good-byes and I took Reggie to work. It was ten o'clock when I walked in. Right on time to open.

"So this is where the queen performs her normal duties," he said.

I plopped him down on the couch. "Listen, Reggie, you're going to have to keep a tight lip on things. I can't have you talking around customers. It'll be bad for business. Not to mention I'm not interested in having the witch council appear and flay me or anything."

"Okay, Just Dylan. I will only speak when spoken to."

"Good."

"Or when we're alone."

"Not good."

The bell above the door tinkled. Roman strode in with Boo following.

"Hey," Roman said. "Did I catch you at a good time?"

"Couldn't be better," I said.

"Ah, it's the young Master Bane," Reggie cooed. "And who's this with him?"

Roman glanced from Reggie to me. "I see you've got the Registry."

"I kinda wished I didn't."

"He doesn't get out much," Roman said.

"So I see. He's been talking nonstop since we left Milly's."

Richard Bane stood in the entrance as if waiting for me to tell him what to do. "Boo, please sit wherever you'd like."

"Well I'd be happy to. Thank you."

"What's going on?" I said to Roman.

"I actually came because I need the Registry."

"How may I be of assistance? Just Dylan doesn't require my special abilities at the moment."

Roman shot me a questioning glance. I shook my head. "Don't ask."

"I need you to look at this photograph and tell me if you recognize the witch in it."

Reggie happily opened. "Show me the image and I will do what I can."

Roman pulled out the picture of the dead man we'd discovered in the gym. "Do you know him?"

The pages flittered right and left. "Let me see. Let me see. He doesn't look familiar, but that doesn't mean his appearance hasn't changed. He has a nice smile. I believe I've seen it before." The pages flapped in a whirlwind.

They stopped.

"Edgar Norwood," Reggie announced.

A similar picture of the dead man appeared. Boo perked up. He came over and peered at the page.

"Edgar Norwood," he whispered. "That's him. That's the man."

"Tell us what you know," Roman said.

Reggie cleared its throat. "Edgar Norwood." He cleared his throat again. "Edgar Norwood," he started.

"What is it?" I said. "What's wrong?"

The book paused. "There's nothing wrong. My page on Edgar Norwood is blank."

"So that means…" Roman said.

Reggie tilted toward us. "Everything about Edgar Norwood has been erased."

FIVE

"Who would have erased it?" I said.

"It isn't would. It's could," Roman said, resting his chin on his fist. "There's only one group I know powerful enough to pull off something like that."

"Who?" I said.

"The council," Boo replied.

We both stared at his father. There were gaping canyons in Boo's memory, so whenever he erupted with a gem of an idea, it shocked me. I think it did the same to Roman.

Boo slid his fingers over his mouth. "The council's the only ones who could do it. Erase someone from the Registry."

"What do you think?" I asked.

Roman scratched the back of his head. "Sounds about right. I might need to pay a visit to them. Or at least to one in particular."

"Who?"

"Gladiolas," he said.

I clasped my hands together. "Oh, I want to come. Can you take me?"

Roman frowned. "Dylan, you're a civilian. This is police

business."

I toed the floor. "I know. But remember when I was queen you said I could have access to information that other folks couldn't?"

"That was when you were queen."

"But this involves witchy things. I might be queen again someday."

He fisted his hips. "Who's going to watch the shop?"

"I've been training Reid."

"I thought she had college classes?"

My baby sister had been taking some community college classes in the basics while she figured out what she wanted to do with her life.

"She has lots of free time with her schedule."

Roman quirked a brow. "And you trust her?"

I shrugged. "More than I trust a stranger."

He closed Reggie and hoisted it under his arm. "Come on."

The three of us left. I snagged Reid from Sera's bakery and promised her an extra fifty bucks to watch the shop alone.

Dewy Dewberry was outside her store when we rolled down the street.

She waved.

***

We parked outside my house. "What are we doing here?" I said.

Roman opened his door. "Gladiolas lives three hundred miles away. It's too far to drive."

"So how are we going to get there?"

"Your grandmother's going to transport us."

I curled my fingers into his shirt. "Are you serious? Every

time she zips us to another place, she always jokes about leaving heads and feet behind. Thing is, I don't think she's joking."

Roman gently pulled my claws off him. "Come on. It'll be quick."

I tried to protest, but it didn't do any good. Next thing I knew the three of us were standing in front of my grandmother. Her hands were raised.

"No one move. I hate for your feet or head to get left here."

I shot Roman a scalding glance. "See?"

He shrugged. "It's a transporting joke. We'll be fine."

A blip and a bump later and the three of us stood in front of an old stone house. Gargoyles sat posted on rails on either side of the wide steps. Spanish tile butted up to the gray stone facing. It was a strange match, but it worked.

"Where are we?" I said.

"Gladiolas likes to keep her whereabouts a secret."

"So you're not allowed to say."

He glanced down at me and smiled. "Darlin', I'd tell you if I could. No doubt about it."

We reached the door and rang the bell. A second later Councilwoman Gladiolas answered.

She wore a beige pantsuit with a black silk shirt underneath. Her brown hair was short except for the bush of bang in the front. Gray streaked the brown. Her eyes widened when she saw us.

"Roman, Dylan. Come in." She took Boo's hands. "Richard, I'm glad to see you're well."

Boo nodded. "Getting there."

She gave him a sad smile. "I know what a delicate situation it is that you're in."

He smiled. "Thank you."

Okay, so outside of a few people, no one knew that Richard

Bane had resurfaced and was living in Silver Springs. Since Boo had disappeared the night of his wife and daughters' killings, the rumor was that he was guilty of the crimes—something Roman had never believed. Since Boo seemed to be suffering from a twenty-year stint of amnesia, Gladiolas and a few other people had decided it was best to keep his reappearance a secret. For now, all was good. But at some point Boo's luck would run out. He would have to answer questions.

Gladiolas ushered us inside her parlor. She offered us coffee, which we all accepted. Once we were comfortable, Gladiolas glanced at Roman.

"You have Reggie with you."

Roman nodded. "I wanted to show you something interesting we found. Reggie. Tell the councilwoman about Edgar Norwood."

Book recited the information in that James Earl Jones voice of his—which was that the page was blank.

"And you found this witch dead in Silver Springs," Gladiolas said.

"As a doornail," Roman replied. "My question is, who would erase his information?"

Gladiolas saucered her cup. "I don't know. But luckily we've got his name and we know he was a witch."

"But it doesn't get us any closer to why he was murdered." I glanced over at Roman. "He was murdered, wasn't he?"

Oops. I'd forgotten to ask.

"Strangled," Roman said.

"So you have a strangled witch," Gladiolas said.

"Who my father recognizes," Roman added.

Gladiolas's gaze zeroed in on Boo. "You knew him?"

Boo glanced at the floor. "I remember the face. Can't tell you where I knew him from, but there was something familiar about him."

"Richard," Gladiolas said, "how would you feel if I tried to retrieve your memory of Norwood?"

Boo took off his hat and dusted the brim. "I don't know."

"If you only focus on the image of Norwood, it will limit the memories that surface. I won't be able to see anything about Catherine. To be honest, I don't want to. Given your fragile state, if I yanked out the wrong memory, one you're not ready to face, it could be cataclysmic for you—your psyche could fracture."

Boo glanced at the floor and sighed. "If you think it'll help."

Gladiolas moved to a lightly stained side table and opened one of the drawers. She pulled out a magnifying glass. "I will investigate each individual memory, choosing to retrieve only those that are relevant. A single memory may, in fact, trigger more."

She sat and twirled the glass between two fingers. "If you want to know your relationship with Edgar, I can find that. It may help your son solve this crime."

Boo nodded. "All right. You can do it."

Gladiolas nodded. "Roman, I want you and Dylan to step back a little bit. Sometimes the process can be jarring. In case Richard lashes out or becomes violent, I want you both out of his reach."

Violent? That didn't sound good.

I backed off, being sure to place Roman in front so that he could defend me if it came down to it. Hopefully it wouldn't come to anything even remotely near that.

Gladiolas placed the glass over Boo's head and proceeded to pick through his hair. It reminded me of primate grooming time at the zoo. I was waiting for her to find a flea and eat it.

I giggled.

Roman stiffened. He threw a glance back at me.

I pressed my lips into a grim line.

Gladiolas looked for several minutes. Finally she stopped right about his left ear. "Ah. Here it is."

She wiggled her finger into the spot. Boo's mouth dropped open. He squirmed.

"This might be slightly uncomfortable." Gladiolas pressed into his head. "Do you remember what happened?"

Boo rolled back his shoulders. "The doorbell rang at Roman's cabin. I answered it. A man stood there. He had dark hair, kind eyes. Said he'd let me down but was going to make it up to me. But he also warned me to be careful. They knew about me and were coming. If they found me, I wouldn't survive."

Boo sanded a calloused hand over his brow. "I don't remember anything after that."

I glanced at Gladiolas. "So who was the man?"

She stepped away from Boo and held out the glass. "See for yourself."

The images of Boo's story played out on the glass. Without the sound, of course. But it was exactly as he said. Edgar arrived. Told him something, and then effectively knocked Boo out.

I nibbled the edge of my finger. "So Edgar showed up to warn Boo that someone was coming for him. Why? Why wait until now?"

Roman's face darkened. "Because someone knows he's out of hiding. Someone wants him dead."

***

We left Gladiolas, and I dragged Roman back to my dress

shop so I could put out a few new pieces. He watched while I worked.

"So why would someone want your father dead?" I said.

Roman stretched out on the couch. "He doesn't remember what happened the night my mother and sisters were murdered. I don't think that's a mistake. I think someone made him forget."

I hooked a dress onto a rack. "But why not just kill him? Why leave him alive?"

He yanked a pillow out from under him, secured it atop his chest and drummed his fingers on it. "I don't know. That confuses me too. Unless—"

"Unless what?"

His eyes sparkled with an idea. "Unless they needed him alive."

I sat down. "You think someone's been protecting him this whole time?"

Roman stopped thumping the pillow. "I don't know but it makes sense. I mean, why not just kill him? Why leave him alive?"

"But when your mother was murdered, she wasn't an ordinary witch. She was Queen. That would've made her murder high treason or something, right?"

His lip coiled. "Pretty sure you're right on that one." He rose, stretched. His T-shirt lifted over his belly, revealing not only stone-chiseled abs but also the dragon tattoo that snaked up the left side of his body. I wanted to reach out and touch it.

Roman caught me staring. "Why don't you?"

I blinked. "Don't I what?"

"Touch it. It won't bite. At least not now."

I giggled. "I don't know; it might." I traced my fingers over the line of the tail.

Roman shuddered. "Darlin', you better watch what you're doing with that hand of yours."

My face warmed. "You dared me to do it."

"I want to dare you to do a lot more."

He pulled me against him and sealed his lips to mine. Heat surged down my spine, and my nerve endings fired electricity. The tingle spread from my chest down to parts unknown.

The kiss deepened. I threaded my fingers through his hair. Roman slid his hands down my waist. His fingers curled under my shirt and sluiced over my stomach. I quivered.

He broke the kiss. Roman's breath came hot, heavy. "Darlin', what you do to me."

"He, he," I said. "Not trying on purpose."

"You don't have to try on accident. Doesn't matter. It happens."

He pulled back and smiled.

An overwhelming wave of emotion rushed over me. I felt it—the gush of joy, of elation, of…love?

Yes, I do believe it was love.

I gulped. "Roman, I know I've been pretty tight-lipped about my feelings."

"No. I like hearing 'right back at you.'"

I poked his chest. "No, you don't. But you're too nice to say anything."

"Nice doesn't have anything to do with it." Truth flickered in his green eyes.

"Well, okay. But you've been more than truthful with your feelings. It's time I told you mine."

He smirked. "Is Dylan Apel about to admit something that makes her vulnerable?"

I rolled my eyes. "I'm trying to open up here."

"I'll shut up."

"Thank you. Anyway, I wanted to tell you that I—"

The door burst open. Reid stood there, purse in hand. "Dylan! We have to go!"

I flashed her a why-the-heck-are-you-interrupting-me-this-better-be-good look. "What are you talking about?"

"The Valentine's Dance. It starts in a couple of hours. Or have you forgotten?"

"No," I seethed. "I haven't forgotten."

I had. I don't know; the whole dead-body thing had thrown me for a loop the past couple of days.

"Grandma wants us there right now."

I pulled away from Roman and shot him an embarrassed smile. "Why?"

"Because she invited Titus the unicorn king as the special guest."

"What! He can't be here! He's a unicorn. We could get in serious trouble for this."

Titus, King of the Unicorns, held a special place in my heart. He was near and dear because he helped me believe in my magic. However, as much as I cared about him, if the witch council discovered my family was showing off a magical creature to nonmagics, I was pretty sure we'd be toast.

Reid tapped her foot. "I tried to tell her it's a crazy idea. So you coming?"

I shouldered my purse and turned to Roman. "Look, I'm sorry. Can I catch up with you later?"

He nodded. "Save me one dance?"

I smiled. "I'll save you the best one."

We headed for the door. My sisters and I might have immunity from the council when it came to working magic in front of regular people, but I was pretty sure showing off a unicorn was not on that list.

"Let's go," I said. "Before she gets us all boiled alive."

SIX

We arrived at the junior high school. Since a dead body had been discovered in the high school gym, the town dance had been moved to the next biggest venue that wasn't a church. We didn't have it decorated to the nines, but it would do with the little bit of crepe paper and hearts that hung from the ceiling.

We dashed inside, carving a path through the maze of the school. We reached the gym in less than a minute. I shoved open the metal doors and gauged the room. Titus stood off to one side with my grandmother. His white mane and tail shimmered under the festive lights, making him look perfectly regal. He wore an opal secured by a wide silver band across his chest, and someone had tucked pink flowers over his ear.

In a far corner—far, far away from the unicorn—the band was performing a sound check. A crystal ball was spinning from the ceiling. The place looked good, if I had to say so myself.

Hope no more dead bodies showed up.

I approached slowly, unsure of what sort of reception I was going to receive. "Hi, Grandma. Hello, Titus."

Grandma positioned the unicorn so that all our backs were to the band. Hopefully they wouldn't notice his mouth moving.

Well, if they did, I could wipe their memories, as I'd learned the night when Rick was at the house for dinner.

Titus whinnied in my direction. "Dylan Apel, it is good to see you. Last we met you were investigating the murder of one of my kin."

I nodded. "I recall. And you gave me a fake opal that you said would focus my powers."

I swear the horse smiled. "I hope you used it wisely."

"I think Grandma and Milly ate it."

He chuckled as much as I expected a horse could.

Grandma fluffed the ends of her hair. "I was just telling Titus all about the Valentine's holiday. About the magic of love and how we celebrate it."

"That all sounds so romantic," Reid said.

Grandma tapped her cheek. "I said the magic of love, dear. Not actual magic. Try not to get your hopes up. You don't have any magic today, and I doubt you'll have any tomorrow."

Reid threw back her head and sighed. "Why does everyone always have to remind me of that? I know I don't have any. I'm not a moron."

"You're just so forgetful," Grandma said.

As if Reid was the only forgetful one in that conversation.

I butted in. "That's great that you were telling Titus about the holiday and that we're having the dance. But what is he doing here? Titus, I'm not trying to be a Debbie Downer or anything, but I'm pretty sure it's against some rule somewhere for you to be mingling with people."

"I've never seen this rule," he said.

I glanced at Grandma. "Seriously. Is this a rule?"

Grandma wiggled her fingers. "Not that I know of."

"What about the horn?" I asked. "People will notice."

Grandma shrugged. "We'll say it's Hollywood special

effects."

I glanced at Reid. "Get Milly on the phone, will you? Have her come down."

Reid walked away.

I turned back to Titus. "What are you going to do here all night?"

Grandma poked the air. "Oh, we have a great idea. Best idea I've had since I decided to go undercover into the swamp monster's lair dressed as another swamp monster."

I sighed. "Did your disguise work?"

"Of course. I was the best undercover agent the witch police ever had."

"I believe you," I lied.

"But anyway, Titus has offered his services for Valentine's pictures."

I glanced at Titus. "Say what?"

"He's going to allow couples to pose with him," Grandma explained. "They can sit on him or stand beside him for a magical Valentine's experience."

"It'll be a magical something," I muttered.

"Ah! Put it out!"

My neck snapped in Reid's direction. She fanned at her heinie. I squinted, trying to see why.

It was on fire.

I shot across the floor.

I smacked her bottoms until the flames were out. I grabbed her arm. "Are you okay?"

She shivered. "Yeah."

"What happened?"

Reid twisted a strand of hair around her finger. "I don't know. I was standing here about to call Milly. I had my phone in my pocket and when I reached down to grab it, I saw my jeans were on fire."

"Okay," I said slowly. "As long as you're okay, I guess everything's fine. But don't keep your phone in your pocket anymore."

"No problem. I won't. Let me call Milly."

"Does your phone still work?"

Reid punched the number and put the phone to her ear. "Seems to."

Ten minutes later Milly arrived. She took one look at Titus and burst into laughter.

"It's really not funny," I said. "We could get into serious trouble for this."

She dismissed me with a wave. "Bah. Nonsense. If the unicorn wants to display himself, he'll be the one in trouble. Not you."

I raised my eyebrows at that. "You think so?"

"I know so. You have nothing to do with this. The council won't bother you. Lighten up, toots. Get in the mood for a little romance."

I sighed. "Fine. I've only got about an hour before folks start to arrive."

I went and found Reid. "Milly seems to think we won't be held accountable for Titus's presence. Not sure how that's going to actually play out, but I'm game." I yawned. "I'm going home to get ready."

Reid nodded. "I'll go with you. We've got to help Sera bring back a whole bunch of desserts, remember?"

I groaned. I loved carpooling food. Not really. "I forgot. Come one."

I waved to Titus and Grandma, who looked deep in conversation. I glanced at the band. None of them seemed to notice. Boy, I hoped the unicorn stopped talking when the guests arrived or we'd have a real problem on our hands.

After I got home and showered, I changed into my royal-blue gown. I'd created it especially for the dance, and the silk slid over my body like melted butter. It felt a little silly dressing up for what was basically a high school dance, but hey, a girl needed a reason to have a little sparkle in her life, right?

As soon as all my clasps were fastened in place, I helped my sisters load boxes of cream puffs into my car and we headed back to the gym.

"That was really weird about my phone catching fire," Reid said. "Do y'all think I have a magnetic behind or something?"

"Pretty sure your rear end isn't magnetic," Sera said.

"You don't know that," Reid said tartly. "It might be my special power."

"To have a magnetic field around your butt?" I cackled. "I hope not. I don't think you'll enjoy that as much as you think."

"I think you're wrong," she said.

"Did you Google it? See if that phone has a problem catching fire?" I asked.

"Yeah," Sera added. "It might be a battery issue or something."

Reid tugged at her hair. "I looked it up, but I didn't see anything about that."

"Well, it was probably nothing," I said.

When we got back to the gym people were starting to arrive. I crossed my fingers and hoped none of them had experienced a conversation with a talking unicorn.

I spotted Titus as we carried in our load of desserts. A woman in a ball gown sat atop him as her date leaned his hand against the unicorn king's shoulder. The professional photographer my grandmother had hired was shooting the scene.

This was going to be an interesting night. As long as the unicorn didn't talk, we should be good.

An hour later the party was in full swing. While I busied myself keeping the refreshment table full, the band played and people danced.

Seriously it was like prom for adults.

"Care to take a five-minute break?"

I looked up and saw Roman. My tongue flip-flopped at the sight of him. He was dressed in a white shirt, black suit and, of course, the tie. His sun-streaked hair was pulled back, and his biceps tugged on the seams of his jacket. The man was a walking cloud of testosterone.

My breath caught. "You look gorgeous," I whispered.

"Not as gorgeous as you," he said, sliding between me and the table. Roman grazed a hand around my waist and nuzzled my neck. Lightning shot down my spine. "So are you going to take me up on my offer?"

"I promised you a dance," I murmured.

"We'll come back to that," he said. "Think you could slip away for a few minutes?"

I glanced at the table. It was stocked solid. "Sure."

"Grab your coat."

He helped me into my wrap, and we exited out a side door. The wind had died down, leaving a tolerably cool night.

"How's that tie treating you?" I asked.

"Great," Roman said. "I wish you'd made me something to wear before now."

I glanced at him, unsure if he was serious or not. "Really?"

"Yeah. This thing's great. I haven't taken it off all week."

I narrowed my eyes. "Yes, you have. You weren't wearing it earlier."

His brows shot up. "Not around my neck, I wasn't," he said

suggestively.

I elbowed his waist. "Quit. You're kidding."

Roman chuckled and wrapped a hand around my middle. "Yes. But if I could wear it all the time, I would."

I smiled and leaned into him, reveling in his body heat.

"I wanted to give you something," Roman said, reaching into his coat pocket.

I gazed up at him. "You didn't have to get me anything."

He rolled his eyes. "Right. The last girl who said that came after me with a switchblade when I took her at her word."

"Whoa. You sure that's all you did to deserve it?"

He shrugged. "I might have broken up with her the same day."

"That sounds more reasonable."

He cocked his head back. "Remind me not to ask your opinion of what's reasonable. Pretty sure that behavior was far from it."

"You broke her heart, Roman. She went psycho for you. It's almost cute."

He stopped walking and faced me. "Let me give you this before I change my mind about where our relationship is heading."

I gnawed my bottom lip. "Great. Now I can take this present and run."

He chuckled. "I had a hard time coming up with something that would beat your necklace, but I think I did it."

I beamed. "Awesome! I've been needing a million dollars."

"Oh, you guessed it."

Roman handed me a small, flat box. "Crap, I was wrong."

"You won't know until you open it," he baited.

I flashed him an innocent smile and yanked off the ribbon. Underneath lay a velvet box. I opened the lid and saw a pair of gold heart earrings. They matched the one around my neck.

"Oh my gosh, they're beautiful," I said.

"Do you like them?"

I clutched the box to my chest. "I love them!" I threw my arms around his neck. Roman lifted me off the ground and spun me around. He planted a long kiss on my lips. I melted into him, smiling as we parted.

"Here. Hold them a minute." I shoved the box in his hand and unhooked the hoops in my ears. I quickly changed them out for the new earrings. "How do they look?"

Roman gave me a smile full of tenderness. "They're pretty, but not as beautiful as you."

"Thank you."

"No," he murmured, nuzzling my ear. "Thank you. For everything."

We went back inside and danced to some song that I didn't know the name of. It didn't matter. The important thing was that Roman held me. I looked into his eyes and felt a swell of emotion. This was love. It was definitely love, and I needed to tell him. I had to tell him. I wanted to tell him.

So just tell him.

"Roman, I want to tell you something," I said, hoisting up my courage and screwing it to some sort of tacky place in my body.

"Hmm?" he murmured. "Is this what you were going to tell me earlier?"

"Um. Yes," I said.

He brought my knuckles to his face and traced them over his lips. I shuddered. "I'm all yours, darlin'."

"I wanted to tell you that—"

"Dylan, the dessert table needs help." Sera stuck her head between us. "Sorry, but I've got my hands full grabbing chairs for the folks from the nursing home." She shot me an embarrassed grin. "Do you mind?"

I shook my head. "No. I'll do it." I gave Roman a feeble smile. "I'll be right back."

I found the extra desserts and started putting them out.

"I'm totally so excited y'all are having this party. Mmm hmm."

My gaze lifted. I didn't want to look, really I didn't, because I knew who owned that voice. But I had to be polite.

Standing on the other side of the table was Dewy Dewberry. She wore a black wrap dress that accentuated her bust and waist. She tugged at a crimson scarf draped around her neck.

"How're you?" I asked, not caring.

She smiled wickedly. Those eyes of hers were big and bright. "Great. The shop should totally open in a few days. Mmm hmm. I already have women peeking in, seeing what I have that's different from the same old they're used to."

That stung. Pretty sure that barb was meant for me and my clothes.

Dewy leaned over. She smacked her lips. "So. I see you've got the unicorn."

I laughed nervously. "Yeah. He wants to be here."

She gave me a tight smile. "Totally hope the council doesn't find out."

A sick feeling filled my belly. "Yeah. Well. We figured since he wants to show himself, he'll be the one in trouble."

"Yeah, I'd hate for the Apels to get in trouble for something. Mmm hmm."

I narrowed my gaze. "We haven't done anything wrong. Who are you, the witch police?"

Dewy glanced away. She cocked her head toward Roman. "I totally felt so bad for you after Jenny mentioned what happened with that one boyfriend of yours. Men can be so awful. What was his name?" She snapped her fingers. "Colten! That was it."

Anger burned in my stomach. This woman knew nothing about me. Nothing. She had no right to drudge up a past that wasn't even hers.

"When I heard that story, I was reminded of a boy who'd done something similar to me."

"Were you boobs involved?" I asked.

"What?"

"Never mind."

"Anyway, what was I totally saying? Oh right, there was this one guy. Viciously handsome. Dangerously cool. I mean he was super hot. He was so hot you could stick a match next to him and it would automatically flame. I mean smoking."

"I get it," I said.

She opened her eyes wide in that deer-in-headlights look. "All the girls drooled over him. I wasn't any different. Would've killed to get a date with him. Then I did." She laughed. "Not kill, but got a date. Had lots of dates with him. Guy told me he loved me. Thought I loved him, too. So I gave him my heart and everything that went with it." She lifted a cream puff to her lips and licked some whip off the top. "Know what he did? Totally dumped me right on my tush."

Her eyes narrowed to wedges. Dewy's face darkened. Power crackled around her.

I took a teensy step back. I glanced around to see if anyone else had noticed, but no one was looking in our direction.

Dewy clenched her fists. "After he dumped me, I totally made a decision not to ever, and I mean ever, be used by a man again. Mmm hmm. That's when I put all my magic into my clothes, giving me the control—not them."

"That's good to know," I said. "Good luck with that."

She shook her head as if snapping out of a trance. The power simmering around her faded. "I let one man have power over me. One man. And one was enough to teach me the lesson that none of them deserve it."

"Okay, great. Well, thanks for the info. It's been enlightening," I said. "But I've got to keep up with the desserts here, or else I'll have a horde of angry Valentine's guests."

Dewy grabbed me by the shoulders and pulled toward her. I batted at her hand. "What?"

"Don't let one man win. They never deserve it."

"Before, you were saying if you had Roman, you'd be telling him you loved him."

"Oh. Ha-ha. Life's full of contradictions, Dylan. That's totally how things are." Dewy released me. She tightened the red scarf around her neck and walked away.

Good riddance.

Sera sidled up beside me. "What was that about?"

"It was about some psycho dolling out love advice."

Sera scooped some of the desserts out of a box and displayed them on the table. "Love advice from the seductress? That's classic."

"Yeah, I know." I put a cream puff on the table and immediately started chewing my nails.

Sera eyed me. "She really got to you, huh?"

I shrugged. "No. Of course not." I paused. "Maybe." I threw up my hands. "I don't know. Sheesh. It was weird. The whole thing. She's weird. Gives me the heebie-jeebies. I wish she'd never moved into town."

"Maybe we can curse her or something and she'll leave."

I perked up at that. "Do you think Milly would teach us a good one?"

"I doubt it."

"Oh."

Sera took me by the shoulders. "Listen, you don't have anything to worry about. That lady's nuts and not worth your time. Anyway, I interrupted your dance with Roman. Don't you have a date to finish?"

Oh my gosh! I was about to utter those three little words in his ear. "Yes! I need to go."

I dropped a cream puff to the table and swung around. My gaze sliced through the crowd as I looked for Roman. Finally I saw him with his back to me. As I waded through the gym floor, my heels clicking on the glossy surface, he slowly turned around.

I was halfway to him when I stopped. The taste of metal filled my mouth, and I gasped for air.

Dewy Dewberry was talking to Roman. But she wasn't just talking. She had her red scarf wrapped around his neck. A sick grin warped her face. Roman's face held no expression. He looked like a blank canvas waiting to be painted.

Holy crap.

Dewy Dewberry was seducing Roman.

SEVEN

If Dewy had worked magic on Roman, I needed to get in there and do something about it—break that darned spell. I took a step forward, but someone grabbed my dress, stopping me.

"Let go." I glanced back and came face-to-face with Titus.

I stared at the unicorn. His black eyes watched me patiently. I spoke through one side of my mouth, doing my best to appear inconspicuous. You know, like I wasn't standing in the middle of a Valentine's Day dance talking to a unicorn.

"I didn't notice you come over here," I said.

He bobbed his head up and down before releasing my dress. "Hers is a twisted heart. One that is bent and hard as stone."

"What?"

"Come outside," he said in a low whisper.

"But Roman," I said.

Titus moved his head from side to side as if watching to make sure no one was looking. "As I said, hers is a twisted heart."

Okay. He could stop being so cryptic now. "I thought we agreed you weren't going to talk."

"That was before I saw the baby stealer," he whispered.

"Baby stealer? Oh, you mean Dewy."

"The baby stealer," he repeated. "That's what we call her."

I led Titus toward a side door. As I crossed the floor, I looked for Roman, but he was gone. So was Dewy. A sinking feeling spread over my belly. I did my best to ignore it, but it pitted my stomach.

When we were completely alone in the cold, I said, "Tell me what happened. I knew she stole a baby unicorn, but that's all the information I have."

Titus whinnied. "Five years ago that woman snuck into Fairyland and took one of the young. Luckily we realized quickly he was missing and sounded the alarm. When we found the witch, she had a blade in her hand and was preparing to steal his horn."

I blew on my hands to warm them. "Reggie didn't tell us that part."

"Only a few of us know what really happened."

"So she was going to steal the unicorn's magic."

Titus nickered. "There's not a shred of doubt in my mind. That woman is evil."

"Evil enough to kill?" I said, quirking an eyebrow.

"Evil enough to kill a baby."

A shudder swept down my body. The words vibrated in my core. If someone was evil enough to kill a baby, there probably wasn't much they weren't capable of.

"As I said, her heart is a twisted thing."

I cocked a brow. "What does that mean?"

Titus bobbed his head. "It means I can see her heart."

I paused. Unsure how to take that. "You can?"

His black eyes sparkled in the streetlights. "It is barbed and twisted from pain—some of it done to her, some of it self-inflicted. It is a heart so wounded I doubt it will ever recover and become the thing of beauty it was at birth."

"Okay, you lost me." I scratched a spot behind my ear. "You can see what a person's heart looks like?"

"All unicorns can."

"All of them?"

He nodded. "Hers is so mangled that Roman's heart should easily know it."

"Roman's heart?"

Titus nodded again.

I wanted to ask, to desperately know what Roman's heart looked like. Should I ask? Turned out, I didn't have to.

"His is guarded. A band runs over it, shielding it. But there is a lock to open it. For all that Roman Bane has been through, the muscle of life of his heart is unscarred."

I scrunched up my face. "So his heart knows that Dewy's isn't good?"

"A true heart recognizes a dark one intuitively. As your heart knows that Roman's is good."

I smiled. "I do know that Roman is good."

"So does your heart."

"May I ask what mine looks like?"

Titus pawed the ground. "You may ask, but I cannot tell you. It is for you to discover the truth of your own heart."

"Oh," I said, disappointed.

"But I will say one thing."

I glanced at him, hope swelling in my chest. "Yes?"

"Your heart can unlock Roman's if you let it."

I narrowed my eyes. "How?"

"That, I cannot tell you. It is for you to figure out."

Oh well, I guess one couldn't just have the mysteries of the universe handed to them. Shucks. "Thank you for that information, Titus. I'll walk you back inside."

We stepped through the door into a whirlwind of commotion.

"I saw you! I saw you do it!"

A woman stood with her purse in hand, beating it over a man's head.

The man shielded himself. "Honey, I didn't do anything!"

"I saw you look at her!"

Not far away stood Dewy. Oh, I wondered who the woman could possibly be talking about?

Just kidding. The woman raised her purse again. It snagged a cluster of streamers overhead, sending the decorations sagging to the floor.

Roman saw me and strode over. I stiffened.

"Well," he said. "Looks like this party's over."

I inspected him, looking for some clue of something, like maybe Dewy had marked him with a big black X on his cheek. Or his crotch. On first glance I didn't see anything.

"Yep, looks like this Valentine's Day is done."

He flashed me a perfect smile. "What was it you wanted to tell me?"

Right. So much had happened, I'd almost forgotten what I was going to tell Roman. Of course now didn't seem like the right time.

I waved my hand. "Oh, nothing," I said dismissively. "You feeling okay?"

Roman grinned. "Never better."

That's what I was afraid of.

***

The next morning was Sunday, which meant I stayed in my

pajamas for most of it. Milly knocked on the door about ten, which was a bit early for my taste, but there wasn't much I could do about it.

She wore a shapeless brown cardigan under her coat. Her normal frown looked deeper than usual.

"I came to get Reggie. It doesn't need to be out of my house for too long."

I crossed to the coffee table where it had been living. "Why's that?"

Nan walked in holding a mug of hot coffee. She sat on the couch. "Because Milly gets to keep him because she was once Queen Witch. He's not supposed to leave her house."

"Oh. Could we get in trouble?"

Milly caned over to the sidebar where we kept the coffeepot simmering on Sundays, and poured herself a cup. She cackled. "Toots, if I got in trouble for everything I've done, I'd be on the registry of bad witches."

I frowned. "Not sure how I feel about that."

Milly grinned. "I'm joking, but I do need to get it back."

Reggie opened. Pages flapped back and forth. "I'm thinking about staying," boomed the voice.

"If anyone discovered you were gone, I'd be in big trouble," Milly said.

Grandma entered. "It would put the council in a tizzy. They'd be pulling out their hair and making wigs with it."

Reggie yawned. "I need a vacation. It's been too long. Besides, you might require my vast knowledge to assist in your murder investigation."

That seemed like a good point. Maybe he could help.

"And it appears the Apel sisters need to learn some magic," Reggie added.

I smirked. "Have you been eavesdropping?"

"I don't know what would make you ask that," he said.

"Because Milly's always coming up with spells for us to learn," I said. "Seems to me you might've been listening to our conversations."

"I am the official Registry of Witches. I don't need to eavesdrop."

"But you did."

"Maybe."

Sera and Reid entered the living room. "What's going on?" Reid said, plopping down in a chair.

"Reggie wants us to learn a new spell," I said.

"Awesome. I'm more than ready."

"Ah, ah, ah," he chided. "Not you. Only the sisters with powers."

Reid crossed her arms. "Crap."

Sera poured herself a cup of coffee. "What spell should we learn today? How to make it rain frogs? How to see into the future?"

"I like that second one," I said. "Count me in."

Reggie thumped his pages back and forth. "How about a truth serum spell."

Grandma clapped her hands. "There's nothing like a good truth spell. Why, I remember one time a hooty owl was refusing to tell me which way the snaggletoothed tiger had gone. I sprinkled a little truth on him and before you know it, I had that tiger pinned by his toes."

I sipped my coffee. "Then we know this spell must work."

Sera smirked but said nothing.

"Milly," I said, "are you going to teach us?"

Milly squeezed the head of her cane. "How about we teach you together? Would that be all right with you, Reggie?"

"Sounds deliciously delightful."

Milly clapped a hand against her thigh. "In most spells, you only need to focus and make the magic work. In a truth spell, you must be physically close enough that you can yank the truth right out of the person's head."

"Like how close?" Sera said. "A few inches?"

Reggie curled up the edges of his cover. "Centimeters work better than inches."

"Okay, so a hairbreadth," I said.

"That'll do. The better you get at the spell, the farther away you can stand," Grandma said.

Sera brushed some lint off her shirt. "But for now I'll jump on my prey and hold them down."

"Precisely," he boomed.

"Let's work it out," Milly said. "Reid, do you want to be the guinea pig?"

"Sure," she said. "It's about all I'm good for."

I patted her arm when she walked past. "Don't be so down, little sis. We all love you."

"Thanks," she said cheerfully.

"Most of the time," I added.

She stuck her tongue out.

Milly turned to me. "Now, Dylan, focus on the question you want to ask Reid. Got it?"

A thought immediately came to mind. I clicked my tongue. "Got it."

"Good. In a moment you're going to ask your question out loud. When you do, you need to tap Reid either on her head or on her chest. Focus on the truth and tap her. Understand?"

"Yes."

"Do it."

I shook out my hands and focused. I felt magic coil in my stomach. It felt good, like an old friend. After a deep inhale I said, "Reid, tell me why you're dating Rick. Because he's really been a douchebag lately."

Her mouth started to drop in shock, but I poked her forehead. A ripple of blue magic flooded from my finger over her body. It shimmered before disappearing in a plume of vapor.

Reid's eyes glazed over. "He only turned into a douchebag lately. He used to be so cool. I'm staying with him because I'm afraid of losing him."

The ripple dissolved, and Reid rubbed her head. She looked at us. "Did you do it? Did you ask me a question?"

"I sure did."

"I don't remember," she said.

"Good thing," Sera said.

I shot her a shut-it look.

Reid glared at me. "Why? What'd you ask?"

I shrugged. "Nothing. Not a thing." I quickly pivoted to Milly. "So is that how it's done? They forget they were ever asked a question?"

Milly smiled. "Exactly. That's how you get away with doing the spell. Of course, if they find a thread of magic on them within a day or so, they'll know something happened."

Reid pulled a pink wiggly thread from her ear. "You mean, like this one?"

I took the twine between my fingers. "I've been wondering what my threads look like." It was small, hot pink and only about an inch and a half long. It curled into a little ball in my hand. It was, I had to say, quite darling.

Yes, I know I'm weird.

I tipped my hand and let the magical thread fall to the ground, where it became nothing more than another piece of lint ready to be swept up.

"Even if someone finds the thread on them, they still won't remember what happened." Reggie chuckled. "It's a useful spell. One that every witch should know."

"Does every witch know it?" I asked.

"No. Very few. Only those with wonderful teachers like yourselves." He shuffled through his vellum. "Lesson learned."

"Great."

"But you might want to watch who you work it on," Milly said.

I frowned. "What do you mean?"

"It works best on nonmagics."

"We're not supposed to work magic on regular people," Sera said.

Grandma cracked her knuckles. "Then it probably won't be a spell you use too often," she said, throwing a look to Milly.

"What's that look for?" Sera asked.

Grandma shook her head. "What look?"

"The one you gave Milly?"

Grandma fiddled with the scarf around her neck. "It's nothing. Not a thing. Nothing for you to worry about."

A smidge of worry tempted to sneak into my mind. I decided to let it go and returned to drinking my warm cup of joe.

"I still want to know what you asked me," Reid said.

I waved off her concern. "It's not important. It was only a stupid question."

She fisted her hands to her hips. "If it was so stupid, then why don't you tell me?"

I turned to Sera. "Hey, do you need to work from the bakery today?"

She slurped her coffee. "Yeah. There's some prep work I need to do for tomorrow."

"I've got some paperwork to catch up on, too. Want to head

68

out soon?"

Sera rose. "Let me shower and we'll roll on out."

I flashed Reid a grin as I exited the room.

"I'm going to find out what you asked me," she threatened.

"Go for it."

***

We made it to town a short while later. I parked in front of our side-by-side stores, Sinless Confections and Perfect Fit.

"Hey, isn't that Roman's car?"

I followed Sera's finger across the street to Dewy Dewberry's new shop.

My heart crashed to my feet.

"Yep." I unlocked my shop and shoved the door open. "Sure is."

Sera followed me inside. "You think he's interviewing her?"

"I don't know." I giggled uncomfortably. "He could be shagging her."

Sera grabbed my shoulders. "What?"

I wobbled over to a chair and sank down. I told her what I'd seen the night before about the scarf and all that.

"You don't think he'd go for her, do you?"

I gave her my how-stupid-of-a-question-is-that look.

"Her clothes do seduce people," Sera grumbled.

I threw up my hands. "Every time she's around, she talks about how hot Roman is, how she wouldn't let him go if he were hers, and that you can't let a man own you. Next thing I know she's got her scarf wrapped around his neck. What do you think she's up to?"

"Seducing your boyfriend."

I lowered my face into my hands.

Sera placed a comforting hand on my shoulder. "Dylan, I don't think Roman would do that. No matter how hard she tried. He loves you too much."

I sat back. "Yeah, but he doesn't think I love him."

"Oh," she said, realization dawning on her. "He's told you, but you haven't told him?"

"Right."

She clicked her tongue. "Still, Roman's not like that. I don't buy that he's in there seducing her."

I perked up. "Want to go over and find out?"

Sera's eyes widened. "You mean spy on them?"

I rose. "Yes. That's exactly what I mean. Peek through the windows."

"You might get arrested."

"I'll say I tripped and fell onto the glass."

She shrugged. "Works for me."

We stalked across the street. "Let's go around back," I whispered. "That's where the real action is."

Sera rolled her eyes. "Oh Lord."

"You're the one who wanted to come with me."

"I know. I'm already regretting it."

We reached the back door, but there weren't any windows. "Crap," I said.

"Just go around the front," Sera said.

The door swung open. I froze. Roman stepped outside. He wore a black duster that came down to his calves, jeans and sunglasses. He stopped when he saw me.

Dewy came out from behind him. She was wearing a satin bathrobe. The material was thin enough to see she wasn't wearing anything underneath. The toad smirked when she saw me.

"Out for a stroll? It's totally a nice cold day to be out

wandering near people's trash cans, don't you think?" she said.

I stretched. "Yep. Just getting our exercise on. Beautiful winter day. You may want to get back inside before something freezes and falls off."

Dewy frowned. "If there's any other way I can service you—oops, I mean be of service to you, Detective, let me know."

Roman nodded. "Thanks." He didn't turn back to look at her. Instead he stared at me until he heard the door shut behind him.

"What are you doing out here? Going through her garbage?"

"No," I snapped. "I was out walking."

"Behind Main Street."

"It's as good a place as any to get exercise."

"Right." He cocked his head toward Sera. "I see Dylan talked you into her harebrained idea."

"Yep, well listen, I need to get back to the bakery, so I'll see you both later." The words flew from Sera's mouth in one continuing sentence. She dashed off before I had the chance to say good-bye.

"Well, I've got work to do, so I'll see you later," I said.

"What's going on?"

"Nothing," I said innocently. "Not one thing."

Roman took my arm. "I'll walk you back."

I skewered him with my glare. At least I think I did. "I don't need your help to walk anywhere. I'm a big girl, in case you haven't noticed."

I took off across the street. Roman matched my stride. Not that it was hard given he was six-two and I was five-five.

"What's going on?"

"Nothing."

I stepped inside and shrugged out of my coat. Roman shut the door and leaned against the glass. "Darlin', last time a girl said there was nothing going on, about five minutes later she was trying to set my hair on fire."

"Don't give me any ideas."

He slid his glasses to the top of his head. "Don't tell me you're jealous of her."

Anger burned in my core. A volcano of emotion erupted. "Okay, I'm really trying not to be childish and stupid, but last night I saw her wrap her scarf around your neck."

Roman stared at me as if waiting for the punch line. "And?"

Heat crept up my neck. Now, I really felt stupid. "And today you're over there and she's dressed in a piece of paper—a see-through piece of paper, I might add."

He laughed.

"I'm sorry that you think this is all so funny."

"I don't," he said, wiping tears from his eyes.

"Pretty much coulda fooled me."

"Darlin', whatever you think is going on between me and that thing across the street, you can stop it right now."

I perked up. "I can?"

"Yes. There ain't anything going on there."

"But the scarf. She seduces men."

He quirked a brow. "What are you talking about?"

I huffed. "That's her magic power, Roman."

He thought about it for a moment. "I can see that."

"What?"

He chuckled; then he crossed over and stroked my hair. "I know what Dewy does. I've been in this business a long time, remember? But you didn't watch long enough. As soon as she tried that play on me, I pulled the scarf off."

"You did?"

He wrapped a hand around my waist. "You think I'd jeopardize anything we have? Not a chance. Not for the likes of her."

I quirked a brow. "Does that mean you'd jeopardize it for the likes of someone else?"

"Don't twist things. Don't make problems where they don't exist."

I sucked in my cheeks. "Okay." I smiled at him. He kissed the top of my head. "So. What were you doing over there when she just happened to be wearing next to nothing?"

"I'm investigating a murder, if you remember."

"What? Do you think she did it?"

Roman crossed to my desk and sat on the lip of it. "I don't know."

I snapped my fingers. "It all makes sense. A new witch arrives. We find another one dead. The new witch was convicted of trying to kill a baby unicorn. She's a bad, bad person. Let's go arrest her."

Roman held up his hand. "Hold on there, cowboy. There's not enough evidence yet."

"We don't need evidence. We'll get some."

He laughed. "I know you're feeling a little vulnerable with a dress shop opening right across the street, but let's not get ahead of ourselves."

"Okay," I grumbled. "But the dead guy, Edgar Norwood— we don't know anything about him except he's some random guy who likes to warn people they need to watch their backs."

"He's not some random guy."

"He's not?"

"No. There's a reason why he wasn't listed in the registry."

"Why's that?" I asked, perking up.

Roman crossed his arms. "Because he was undercover witch police. Whoever killed him murdered a cop."

EIGHT

My jaw dropped "He was? Why didn't you say that earlier?"

Roman shrugged. "Because I like to keep some secrets for myself."

"Very funny."

"Because I needed to make some calls. Make sure my hunch was right."

"And it was?"

He nodded. "Yes."

"Tell me more."

Roman glanced around the room.

"The room's not bugged. No one can hear us."

"I know."

I nibbled on the tip of my fingernail. "I won't mention it to anyone."

He cocked his head.

"Okay, not to anyone important."

"You can tell Sera and that's all."

"Fine. I don't know why you're suddenly worried about me spilling information. You've told me things before."

"This is sensitive, Dylan. Someone's close by, waiting and

watching."

I glanced out the window. "Where's your dad, by the way? Aren't you worried about him?"

"He's at the station. I dropped him off before coming over here."

"So you're keeping him well protected."

Roman flicked a speck of dirt from his duster. "As best I can without locking him up."

"Okay, shoot."

"Edgar Norwood was an undercover agent for the witch police. That's why his registry page was wiped. I figured as much."

I crossed to my coffee counter and started making a pot. "Why wipe his registry? Why not just make up a fake bio for him?"

"Probably some lazy desk clerk didn't do their job right."

"Okay, go on."

Roman shrugged out of his duster. He draped it across the desk and sat back down. "I contacted a high-ranking official and asked him what he could find out about Edgar. Turns out, the guy's been deep undercover for years. Guess what he's been doing?"

My super amazing coffeepot finished burping and gurgling the last of the liquid. I poured a cup for both of us.

"He's been undercover trying to stop the magic-stealing ring."

"You got it."

I almost dropped my mug. "You're kidding."

"No."

"So what would make him appear now? Why warn your dad?"

Roman sipped the liquid. "He might have been about to

surface. He may have finally figured out who the head honcho is and decided it was time to get out. But first, he wanted to tell my dad to be careful."

"Why?"

Roman shrugged. "Loyalty, maybe? When my mom and sisters were murdered, there was an uproar in the community. People were angry and scared. They protested. Wanted to know who'd done it. Demanded justice for their queen."

"And they never got it," I whispered.

Roman's eyes clouded. "They never did. But one day I'm going to give it to them."

I walked over and kissed his cheek. "You will."

He rubbed his thigh. "I hope so." Roman handed me the cup. "I need to get going. I'll call you later."

"Okay." Lucky for Roman a thousand-watt idea simmered in my head. One that would wrap this whole investigation up in about five minutes.

***

"We need to do the truth serum spell on Dewy," I said to Sera several hours later.

She glanced up from her book. "And you think this is a good idea why?"

"Because she's a wannabe baby unicorn killer."

"What?"

I explained what Titus had told me.

She tucked a strand of glossy dark hair behind one ear. "That's pretty stout stuff, there."

"I know."

"So you think she murdered that dead guy because years ago she was caught about to cut off a unicorn's horn."

"Seems like a logical step from A to B."

Sera laughed. "Dylan, I don't think that's a logical step. I think it is for you, but not for the rest of the world."

My cheeks flamed. "You don't think that makes perfect sense?"

"Not really. But because you're my sister and I love you, I'll help. But this one might backfire."

"What makes you say that?"

Sera shut her book and rested it in her lap. "She's strong, Dylan. And I don't mean just her magic. Dewy seems to have some sort of fire burning inside her that gives her that edge— albeit a ditsy one. She's trouble."

I sat down across from her. "So you're scared."

She smirked. "I'm not scared. But it seems rash. Roman's investigating. Let him do that."

"But he might need help."

"He's a big boy, Dylan. Pretty sure he can take care of this himself. You know, this reminds me of the time I decided Mr. Porter the science teacher needed a puppy. Remember, when I was in sixth grade?"

"Yes. It was so thoughtful."

Sera shook her head. "But it wasn't thoughtful. The man was deathly allergic to animals. Their fur flared his asthma. But I wanted to get him a dog because I thought he was lonely, so I got him a dog."

"You were so sweet."

"You're not listening, are you?" she said.

"Not really."

Sera glared at me.

I rolled my eyes. "Okay, I'm listening. Butt out. That's your sage advice."

"It is."

"Is there any way I could get you to change your mind?"

"No."

A crash came from the other side of the house. It shook the walls and rattled the furniture. I flashed Sera an oh-crap look before flying out the door.

I ran into the living. "What's going on?"

I came to a sliding stop.

In the doorway stood a hooded figure. The cowl of his robe was pulled down so far I couldn't see his face. For that matter, I couldn't actually tell if it was a man or woman, but referring to it as a man just seemed to fit.

Grandma stood in the center of the living room. Her hand was raised. "You will not come in here."

The figure lifted his palm. Black threads of magic streamed toward Grandma. She met his magic with her own pink rays. The streams tangled together.

Bits of magic flew out, smashing into lamps, mirrors, pictures. Glass shattered all around.

Nan appeared from the kitchen. She had a spear in her hand. That's right. A spear. With a sharp metal tip and all. She flung it at the figure. He lifted his free hand, and the spear fell to the floor.

Nan sprang toward him. He wrapped her in a cocoon of power, essentially bubble-packing her. Nan kicked. "I'll have your head!" She stretched and squirmed, but the bubble held her fast.

"Get out of my house," Grandma yelled.

The figure's magic shredded into hers. It was pushing back on Grandma, gaining on her.

I lifted my hand and shot a surge of power at the figure. It knocked him into the doorjamb. He looked in my direction and started to raise a hand toward me.

Another hooded figure appeared behind the first one. This one focused completely on me, sending a stream of magic flooding in my direction. I created a shield, but it was no match for the power bearing down on me. It started to collapse.

Sera sprang up from behind me. She focused her power, strengthening my shield. The moment gave me a chance to glance at Grandma. She still held her own, but none of us were getting anywhere. We were all pushing, but no one was gaining. We needed help.

I glanced at the giant mirror over the buffet.

"Sera, can you hold the shield?"

Sweat ran down her temple. "I'll try."

I pivoted toward the mirror and aimed. The structure lifted from the wall, hovering in the air for half a second before crashing down on the hooded figures, knocking them back.

Everything stopped.

I paused, heaved a huge breath. I nodded to Sera and sprang forward. She followed.

"Dylan, wait," Grandma yelled.

There was no time to wait or think. Our lives were clearly in danger. If I gave those two a moment to recover, we'd be dead by the time they stood up.

I bolted through the door and into the cold night. Shattered glass lay scattered over the ground. The figures were nowhere to be seen. They'd vanished.

My breath turned to steam in the night air. I gulped down some oxygen and collapsed to my knees, my body shaking.

My grandmother laid a hand on my shoulder. "You showed courage, Dylan."

"So did you."

Sera and Reid walked up beside me. Reid carried a massive wok in her arms.

"What's that for?" I asked.

"I was ready to step in if you needed me."

I flashed her a weak smile. "Thanks." I looked up at Sera. "Is your mind changed about the truth spell?"

A grim frown spread over her face. "I think it is."

***

Witch police crawled all over the house. I'd wanted to keep the attack a secret, but Roman wouldn't allow it.

Inspectors combed through everything, looking for clues as to who attacked us.

"You didn't see their faces?" Roman asked.

"No. Their hoods were pulled down too far and they never spoke. They only attacked."

Roman nodded to a young witch policeman who was jotting down notes.

"Well, I see the Apel family is up to mischief once again."

I groaned. I knew the voice all too well.

Jonathan Pearbottom, Inspector not extraordinaire, threw one side of his tweed cape over a shoulder. His parrot nose looked particularly parrot-ish in the moonlight.

"Good to see you too, Inspector."

He gave me curt grin. "It was only a matter of time before someone decided to end your life in a spectacular way. I'm surprised this attack didn't come sooner."

"I'm surprised a baboon doesn't live up your rear end," I said.

Roman snickered.

"What was that?" Pearbottom said.

"Nothing. Believe it or not, I haven't gone around angering witches. At least not that I know of."

Pearbottom looked at Roman. "We've swept the area, but the witches were good. Left no traces of themselves or their power. My men will clear out and leave this in your hands. We'll be in touch."

Roman nodded. "Thanks, Jonathan."

The inspector smirked. "Hopefully this was a one-time occurrence and we won't be called in again." He yanked on his bowler hat and walked away.

Roman turned to me, hands fisted on his hips. "Are you sure you're okay?"

I rubbed a knot on my shoulder. "Fine. Nothing a shot of rubbing alcohol can't fix."

"Very funny."

"A girl's gotta try."

Roman glanced down the street. "Once we erase the neighbor's memories, I'll station either myself or someone else outside. I'll watch the house as much as I can."

"You don't have to do that." I pressed my palm to the center of his chest and quivered at the heat wafting off him.

"Yes, I do. Someone tried to kill you."

I smiled feebly. "We don't know that. They might have just been saying hi."

He frowned. "Don't joke."

"Okay. Fine. It's how I cope with stress."

He wrapped me in a bear hug made of chiseled muscle and said, "I know. It'll be okay."

I melted into Roman and sighed. For once I had a hard time believing him.

***

It was business as usual the next day. I went to work early

and had a few out-of-town customers who'd heard about the store and had decided to make a day trip to Silver Springs. I sold some garments, made some money.

Usually that was enough to put me in good spirits. Today, however, it wasn't.

The bell above the door tinkled.

"Welcome to Perfect Fit," I said. "How can I help you?"

"Well, hello, Miss Dylan." Richard Bane tossed me a worn, tired smile. He shuffled across the floor in heavy-booted feet.

"Boo, what brings you to town? Is Roman with you?"

He shook his head and sank down into a chair. He palmed a face sagging with worry.

"Let me make you some coffee," I said.

"That'll be just fine."

I revved up the percolator and poured two cups. "Where's Roman?" I said, handing him a steaming mug.

"At the station doing some work." His green eyes matched Roman's. Though Boo had a few more crinkle lines in the corners, but there was no doubt who Roman had inherited his eyes from.

I sighed. "You heard about last night."

He tipped the cowboy hat on his head. When we found Boo, he was wearing a raccoon fur hat. Since we'd transitioned him from the wilderness, he'd taken to donning one of the cowboy variety. With his long beard and slow-talking ways, I'd say it suited him.

"I didn't mean to bring this trouble to you."

I pinched my brows together. "This isn't your fault."

He set the cup down and folded his hands in his lap. "I'm afraid it is. I should've stayed well enough hidden. I'd been out in the wilderness so long, I don't know what drew me back."

I shrugged. "Maybe you have a story to tell and you wanted

to let us know."

He pulled out a pocketknife and started cleaning the undersides of his fingernails. "You'd be mistaken if you think I haven't thought about the night Roman's mother was killed every day since I've been back. Not one hour has passed that Catherine's image doesn't drift into my mind." He stopped. "Almost seems unbelievable that when you found me, I couldn't even remember the night she was killed."

I sipped my coffee. "Sometimes the mind works to protect us. Shuts down certain memories so we can go on, keep living."

"I've considered that and it seems reasonable, but I don't think that's it. There's a memory floating in my mind, one just under the surface. One I need to get rid of."

I flexed my fingers. I could tell this was going to be good. "What is it?"

"It's another memory of Edgar. You see I'd met him before that day here. I know it." Boo finished up with his fingernails, folded the blade and slid the knife into his back pocket. He stroked his beard in thought. "I want to say he's the man who made my memory go away."

"Why would he do that?"

Boo shook his head. "Now that, I can't figure out. That's why I need you to find that memory."

"Me?" I laughed. "There are other witches out there more capable than me."

Boo gave me a slow, thoughtful smile. "Ah, yes there are. But you like to know things, Dylan Apel. You like to know a lot of things."

"You mean I'm nosy."

He smiled. The lines etching his cheeks deepened. "I'm a gentleman. I say things a bit nicer than that."

I chuckled. "You got me there. What makes you think I can

do it?"

"You defeated two witches last night. I'm pretty sure you can smuggle a memory from my head."

There really was nothing for me to decide on this. Boo had information. I needed to know things. Simple as that. "When do you want to do it?"

"How about now?"

I grimaced. "As in this very moment?"

"You know a better time?"

"Nope. I guess not." I snapped my fingers. "But I don't have one of those magnifying glass thingies. And don't you want Roman here for this?"

He shook his head. "No. It might be too painful." Then he pulled a magnifying glass from his pocket.

"Where'd you get that?"

He shrugged. "I may or may not have borrowed it from Councilwoman Gladiolas."

I took the glass. My fingers glided over the slick mother-of-pearl handle. "Jeez Louise. I don't want to be anywhere near her when she finds out it's gone."

He patted my hand. "Don't worry. I'll take the rap." He slapped his thigh. "Well, I'm ready when you are."

I shook out my hands and tried to recall exactly how Gladiolas had done her thing with the glass. Since I actually had no idea, I decided winging it would be best. I focused on an image of Edgar as I picked through Boo's hair. I traced over one side, across the top of his forehead and down the other.

To be honest, I didn't see anything except scalp, and I didn't know if I would. I didn't even know if I was doing this whole thing right. All I saw was hair shaft after hair shaft as I swept the glass over his head. I was about to give up when a picture of Edgar popped into view.

"Oh my gosh! I found it."

"Now watch."

The image was dark. It was nighttime, but I couldn't tell exactly where it was. Edgar looked years younger. He had Boo by the scruff of the neck.

"Calm down, Richard. Take a breath."

"But Catherine!"

Edgar shook him. "You can't do anything about it now."

Boo glared at Edgar, his expression darkening. "You. You were with them. You did this!"

"I'm not with them, Richard. I'm going to help you."

Boo's anger melted as he crumpled to the floor. "My wife! My children! I saw her face. The one who held that wand."

Edgar took a step away. He paced back and forth, running his fingers through his hair. "It's too early to expose everything. Much too early." He turned back to Boo. "Richard, I hate to do this to you, but I must." Edgar crossed to him. He placed a thumb and finger on Boo's forehead. "When you wake up, you won't remember any of this. You won't know who you are."

The image went to black.

I dropped the glass. It clattered to the floor.

"What'd you find?" Boo asked.

My fingers trembled and my breath hitched. "The murders— your wife and daughters. You were made to forget."

His voice soured. "What else?"

I steepled my fingers to my mouth. "Edgar Norwood knew all about it."

NINE

"Edgar Norwood erased your father's memory of your mother's murder."

Roman dropped his fish taco. Okay, so maybe I hadn't picked the most perfect time to tell him. You know, it's not easy laying a bomb like that on someone. In fact, I'd been debating how to tell him. Of all the situations that could have occurred, this one seemed like the best option.

He scooped up a grilled filet. "How do you know this?"

"Your dad had me peek into his memories."

Roman winced. "Figures."

I pushed a mound of refried beans with my fork. We sat at the only Mexican joint in town. It was empty thanks to the cold winter night and the fact that Valentine's Day was over. People wanted to be snuggled up in their homes, not out and about. I couldn't blame them.

"What do you mean, 'figures'?"

Roman wiped a napkin over his mouth. "I'm not surprised he had you snooping around. He's carrying a lot of guilt."

"He didn't do anything."

"Did Edgar? Was it him who killed them?"

I shook my head. "No. I don't think so. The memory was foggy, but from what I could see your father knew who did it, but Edgar didn't want him to tell. Said it was too early to expose everything."

Roman sat back. The top edge of the dragon tattoo peeked out the neck of his T-shirt. I stopped myself from reaching out and caressing it.

Roman steepled his hands and placed them under the tip of his nose. "Too soon into the investigation, probably. If Edgar had gone after the murderer, he wouldn't have discovered whatever it was he was sent to do."

I mushed my beans into my rice. "Have you figured out exactly what that is?"

Roman raked both sets of fingers through his hair. He mussed it enough for it to look beach blown. I purred inside. He was hunky, sexy, and all testosterone. Yum.

"No. I've got some calls out. Just waiting to get in contact with the person in charge of Edgar."

I raked my fork through my beans, leaving an imprint of the tines. "Any ideas on who attacked my family?"

He sighed. "I wish I had good news, but no." Roman slid his hand across the table and took mine. "But I'll find them. Whoever it was, they won't remain hidden for long."

I squeezed his palm. "Why us? No offense, but I thought these folks wanted your dad."

Roman smiled sadly. The corners of his eyes crinkled. "I think you've made a name for yourself. In case you haven't noticed, you have a habit of knocking out people involved in magic stealing."

I dumped a glob of queso onto my beans and ate a mouthful. "If they didn't try to kill me first, it wouldn't be a problem."

Roman smiled sadly. "I think you've got someone's

attention."

I pulled back. "I don't want anyone's attention."

"Darlin', there's no choice in this. Until we find the witches and nail them, you're in danger."

I sank my head on the back of the cool, vinyl booth. It was split in a few places, frayed, but you could tell it had good bones.

"I won't let anything happen to you," he said. "You know how I feel."

I rubbed my hands over my face. "Roman, why do you love me? I mean, I can be whiny, I don't always have my act together, and I usually run headfirst into situations without thinking."

"'Cause you're so darn cute."

I glared at him. "Please tell me that's not your real answer."

"What if it was?"

"I'd say you were lying."

He drummed his fingers on the table. "I don't know. Why does anyone love anyone? Because when you're with them, that person makes you better. I'm better with you. You don't always have your feet on the ground, Dylan. That's okay. I do. But that's what I need sometimes. Someone who doesn't take things so seriously, someone who makes me laugh. Someone who makes the world brighter."

I arched a brow. "You're saying I do all that?"

"That and a bucket of chicken more."

I smiled at him. Warmth spread over my face and washed down my body. I wanted to melt into Roman, to forget all the crap going on and just focus on him.

He never pushed. He never shoved. He simply waited patiently. As I held his gaze, the sense of love flowed through me. I felt it on the tip of my tongue. I was going to say it.

The front door swung open. Frigid wind swept across the restaurant, slicing into my skin. I shivered and looked up, wanting to know who'd had the nerve to interrupt my special moment with Roman.

Dewy Dewberry shook off the cold. She spotted us and beamed. She had some guy on her arm. His face was directed away as he hit the alarm on his car. He stayed turned as she dragged him over to our booth.

"Hey, y'all, totally good to see you. Dylan, how are you holding up?" She leaned over. "I heard the terrible news through the grapevine. So sorry. Mmm hmmm. But I'm totally glad everyone's okay." She yanked her date forward. "I think you may remember Colten, right, Dylan? Colten Blacklock?"

My stomach plunged to the tile floor. I swallowed the bowling ball in the back of my throat and glanced up. I met Colten's dark, boyish eyes. His light brown hair was mussed. The dimple in his chin winked at me as it had in high school. His slim build looked perfect in the leather jacket and jeans.

He flashed me a smile full of mischief. "Hey, Dylan. How've you been?"

About a thousand emotions screamed to get out. Anger, humiliation, grief, regret. All of them. Here stood the guy whom I'd given my heart, soul, and other things to in high school. That was right before prom, the night he stood me up. He never showed, and then he had the nerve to tell everyone what he'd done to me. I despised him.

Yes, I realize that was ten years ago and I needed to get the heck over it. But right now, raw emotion tumbled in my gut.

I forced it back down to the sewer of my bowels and put on my biggest smile.

"I thought you'd moved away, Colten."

He shrugged. "I'm visiting my parent for a few days."

"Great. This is my boyfriend, Roman. He's a police officer."

Colten extended his hand. "Nice to meet you."

I knocked Roman's hand away before they could shake. "Honey, Colten has leprosy."

Colten glared at me. "What?"

"Oh, you don't? I'd heard that's why you left Silver Springs."

He sneered at me. "I don't have leprosy."

I grabbed my jacket. "Well, that's too bad. I mean, that's good. Great. So glad you didn't have to move to a leper colony and lose your limbs one by one."

I slid out of the booth. "Listen, we've got to be going. I need my beauty rest if I'm going to run the most successful dress shop in Silver Springs. Great seeing you both. Y'all take care."

Roman pushed out of the booth and followed. He handed the cashier some money. When he opened my car door for me, he said, "So that's the ghost of relationships past."

"I don't know what you're talking about. He's just some guy I haven't seen in a long time."

"Right. And I'm an astrophysicist."

I shrugged. "You could be and I just don't know it."

He grunted.

"Listen, have you checked out Dewy? Don't you think she might have been the one who attacked us?"

"She's got a solid alibi," he said.

"I don't trust her."

"I don't trust many witches except for you."

"I think you should look into her again."

Roman pushed a strand of hair from my eyes. He kissed me long and deep. The tension in my shoulders and neck went slack.

"What was I saying again?" I said.

"You were saying you wanted to go back to my place so I

could guard you naked."

I laughed. "I didn't say that."

He licked his lips. "No, but you were thinking it."

Roman might have been right there.

"As wonderful as that sounds, I need to get back home. I have to stay with my family in case we're attacked again."

He exhaled. "Okay. But the other way sounds like more fun." Roman shut the door and crossed to the driver's side.

"It did," I whispered. But I had plans to make. Plans that didn't involve Roman, because if he knew, he'd kill me.

***

When I got home, the entire house smelled like cinnamon and vanilla. Roman and I entered the kitchen to find Sera surrounded by stacks of cakes. I'm not talking about one or two cakes. There were four stacks piled five high on the counter and two stacks of five on the small tile island.

"Um, what's going on?" I said.

Sera opened the oven and pulled out a golden brown cake. "I'm baking." She shoved the pan on top of the stove and yanked off her mitts.

"I see that. Any reason why?"

She shrugged. "No reason. Just thought I'd burn off some extra energy."

I shot Roman a worried look. "Are you going to eat all of these?"

She shook her head. "No. They're for other folks. I couldn't eat all these in a week if I tried. Roman, I have some for you and your dad right here." Sera grabbed a stack and shoved them into his arms. "Here you go. It's vanilla cake with vanilla icing. I hope you like that."

He nodded. "Smells delicious."

"If that's not enough, I have more. I wasn't sure how many your dad might eat in a day."

"How about one slice?" I suggested.

Sera smirked. "Some people like cake, Dylan."

"Some people want to ward off diabetes, too."

"I don't know what you're talking about."

A knock came from the back door. Sera opened it. Two neighbor kids stood in a pool of lamplight. I was surprised their mother had let them out on a dark and cold night, but Silver Springs was pretty safe. Unless you were me and my family, of course; then witches came out of the woodwork to blast you into tomorrow.

Sera squealed. "Y'all came back. Great! Here's some cakes for you." She handed both boys a stack.

Roman tipped his head toward me. "You got this one?"

I nodded. "I hope so. If not, I'll be swimming in cake batter by tomorrow morning."

He planted a kiss on my forehead and left with his stack of cakes. Sera shut the back door and crossed to her mixing bowl. She started dumping more flour into it.

I grabbed her hand. "Stop. Just stop. You're going to suffocate us."

Sera's lower lip trembled. "But I have to. I have to spread happiness."

"Sit." I dragged her to a chair and pressed her onto it. "What's going on?"

"I don't know. The attack kinda did me in."

I smiled weakly. "It's okay. We'll find out who did it."

"But what if we don't?"

"Do you think baking for the entire town will help?"

She dropped her arms to the table and laid her head square in the center of them. Sera groaned. "I don't know. Yes. I think baking will save the world. If the witches get one of my cakes, maybe they'll forget all about us and won't bother our family again."

I squeezed her arm. "Stinks, doesn't it? Fighting for your life."

"I'm surprised you don't sew more dresses," Sera said.

"I guess I have other ways of dealing with stress. Perk up. I'll tell you something that makes the other night look like a Sunday at Putt-Putt golf."

Sera sniffled and glanced up. "What's that?"

"Dewy Dewberry toted Colten Blacklock into Las Vias tonight."

Sera shot up. "No!"

"She sure did."

"To get to you?"

I shrugged. "I'm assuming so."

"What a witch."

"You got that right."

"Whoa! What's with the vomiting cakes?" Reid stood in the kitchen doorway.

"Sera's decided to join the PTA bake-off."

Reid snapped her neck toward Sera. "Seriously?"

Sera scoffed. "Of course not seriously. That's ridiculous."

"So's that mountain of cakes," Reid said.

"It's therapeutic," Sera said.

Reid trailed her finger over the lip of icing and popped her finger in her mouth. "They're good, though. Might be a bit of crazy cat-lady overkill, but it's tasty."

"Thanks," Sera said.

"Can I have a slice?"

"I thought you were on a diet," Sera said.

Reid shrugged. "I don't feel like it anymore."

I narrowed my eyes. "You don't feel like being on a diet? You've been on one ever since you started dating Rick."

Reid carved out a hunk of cake that was a quarter of its entire size. "I'm just not feeling it."

"Why are you feeding your sorrows?" Sera said.

"Probably for the same reason you're baking yours away," Reid said.

Sera and I exchanged confused glances. "Did you and Rick break up?" I asked.

Reid shrugged. "Maybe."

I tried not to cheer. Instead I rose, crossed to Reid and directed her back to the breakfast nook table. "What's going on?"

Reid sniffled. "Nothing. We decided to take a break." Her sniffles became hiccups and the hiccups, sobs.

"He doesn't want to see me anymore," she wailed.

I grabbed a box of tissues, plucked out about a thousand and handed them to her. She honked her nose. "H-he d-doesn't like me. S-s-says I'm clingy."

Shocker. All Reid ever talked about was how dreamy Rick was. No surprise he found her to be a bit on the static-cling side of things.

"I'm so sorry," I lied.

"He's a jerk. Doesn't know how good you are," Sera said.

"I know you didn't like him," Reid said. "You don't have to lie."

"We used to like him," I said. "He used to be cool. But then you started dating and he made all those jerky comments."

Reid blew her nose. It was loud enough to wake the really, really dead. "I think he was trying to get me to break up with him. He didn't say that, but I think so."

Sera gave her a hug. "Men stink."

"Yes, they do," Reid said. "I'm just going to eat my cake and swallow in my sorrows."

"That's wallow in your sorrows," I said.

"Whatever," she grumbled.

"Listen, I've got something that'll cheer you up."

Reid didn't perk up when she said, "What's that?"

So I told her all about Dewy and Colten.

"She's really trying to get to you," Reid said.

"She's horrible," Sera said. "Think she's trying to sabotage you so that your business tanks?"

I shrugged. "I don't know, but I wish she'd move away."

Sera started cleaning up her baking mess. "Maybe she's trying to get you to leave. You know, make your life stink so that you'll pack up and go."

"Yeah, maybe," I said.

"But I'm sure it wasn't that bad," Reid said. "I mean you dated Colten like a thousand years ago. I'm sure it wasn't so bad seeing him."

My gut twisted. It had hurt, but I didn't have the courage to tell them.

"Dylan, are you still screwed up over him?" Sera said.

I rubbed the back of my neck. "No. Of course not. That was ages ago. I mean, he only broke my heart, took my virginity and then stomped all over my reputation. It's not like it's a big deal or anything."

"And you wonder why no one's put a ring on that finger yet," Reid said.

"I don't wonder that," I snapped.

"I do. But now I know."

"Listen, Colten Blacklock has absolutely nothing to do with why I didn't date anyone before Roman."

Now it was time for Reid and Sera to exchange looks.

"He doesn't," I said feebly.

Sera clapped her hands. "Okay, well, back to Dewy Dewhead. I wish there was some way to get rid of her. Get her out of here before she emotionally scars us for good."

I rubbed my hands together. "Easy. All we need to do is prove that Dewy was one of the witches who attacked us."

Sera quirked a brow. "Do you really think it was her?"

I snatched a crumb of cake off Reid's plate. "Why not? She's a witch. A bad one, at that. And we were attacked by bad witches. Seems like a logical conclusion to make."

Reid smirked. "Not really. But how are we going to do it?"

I shrugged. "We sneak into her house and do the truth serum spell on her before she even knows we're there. We simply ask her if she attacked our house."

Sera dried a plate. "If it were that easy, why didn't the witch police do that?"

"Perhaps I can shed some light on this," said a deep, velvety voice.

Sera and I jumped. "Ah!"

"Sorry," Reid said. She pulled Reggie out of her backpack. "I forgot to tell you I was lugging it around."

Sera clapped a hand over her heart. "For goodness' sake. Next time let us know."

"Sorry," Reid said meekly.

I cracked my knuckles. "Okay, Reggie, illuminate us. Why didn't the witch police use the truth serum on Dewy?"

"The truth serum spell can be—how shall I say—a little tricky."

"How so?"

His pages hummed. "It's not exactly legal."

I smacked my palm to my forehead. "Why would you teach

us an illegal spell?"

"Well, it's not exactly illegal, either. It's not looked on very highly."

"So you taught us a spell we can't use."

"Not true," he said. "It can be, and is used. It's just not one of the go-to spells a witch investigator would use."

"Why's that?" I asked.

"Yeah," Reid chimed. "Why is that?"

"Well," Reggie said, clearing its throat. "There's only one teensy problem with it."

"Yes," I said. "And that is?"

He jumped from Reid's backpack and landed on the table. "The old laws deemed the spell illegal, but that law was replaced. An amendment was made to it, making the spell perfectly legitimate."

"Then why don't the witch police use it?" Sera asked.

"Because if it's used against a witch and the witch realizes it, she can invoke the old law and say the perpetrator used the truth spell on her illegally."

"So what's the punishment for that?" I asked.

"Witch prison," Reggie said. "You'll go away for the rest of your life."

TEN

"Are we still doing this?" Sera asked, wiping crumbs off her face. We'd brought one of the cakes in the car with us. For, you know, courage. I'm not going to lie; I can be a bit of a stress eater. In fact, all of us could be, as proven by Sera.

She tore off a hunk and nibbled on the edge. "Seriously? Are we breaking into Dewy's house and doing this truth spell on her?"

I nodded. "Why not?"

"Because you might go to jail," Reid chirped. "For apparently the rest of your life. Until you're an old, shriveled-up lady who looks like a piece of leather wrapped over bones."

"Thanks," I said.

She beamed from the backseat. "You're welcome. Just giving you something to look forward to."

"How kind."

Sera dropped the chunk of cake into the box, closed the lid and tossed it into the floorboard. "She's right. You could go to jail."

I turned onto Main. "Only if she invokes that old law. What

98

are the chances of that?"

Sera brushed crumbs off her hands. "I don't know. All we know about her is that she likes to talk about how hot your boyfriend is. Oh, and apparently she likes to torture you."

"Exactly. I don't think someone like that would even know the old law."

"You didn't know about it," Reid said.

"That's exactly why I don't think she will, either."

Sera touched my arm. "This is the woman who was going to kill a baby unicorn and somehow got out of it."

"She didn't get out of it. She went to jail."

"So she might know about the law."

I threw up my hands. "The truth spell erases the person's short-term memory. All we have to do is wipe her memory of us being there at all and we'll be in the clear."

Sera tugged on her seat belt. "What if she admits to being one of the witches who attacked us?"

"Then I tell Roman."

"Do you think he'll use it?"

"I hope so. I'll break up with him if he doesn't."

Kidding. I was kidding.

I pulled behind the row of buildings that Dewy's was on. "Apparently she's living above her store."

"How are we going to get in?" Reid said.

Crap. I hadn't thought of that.

"Perhaps I can be of use," Reggie said.

"What's that thing doing here?" I said.

Reid shrugged. "He jumped into my backpack. I thought it might be useful."

I shook my head. Whatever. "Okay, Reg. How can you help us enter her house?"

"I can teach you to sink your hand through the wall and unlatch the lock from the inside."

Well, that was useful.

"Great. Give me the skinny."

"You'll need to imagine you're transparent."

I waited for the punch line. None came. "Is that it?"

"That's it."

"Great. Let's get this show on the road."

"Of course, usually only very high level witches can do that sort of magic."

I groaned. "So is it going to work?"

"Probably not."

"I'll try anyway."

Okay, so I'm not going to lie and say I was totally comfortable breaking and entering. Well, technically I wasn't breaking. Only entering. It was late. I figured Dewy would be asleep. Or at least close to it. I didn't see any lights on, but that didn't mean anything.

We exited the car and slinked over to the door that I'd seen Roman come out of earlier. I nibbled my fingernails for some good old-fashioned luck, placed my palm beside the lock and thought about making my hand thin enough to push through the door.

The light snapped on. The door flew open.

Dewy Dewberry hovered over us. She wore that same stupid flimsy nightgown that would freeze any normal person during winter. Apparently this witch wasn't normal.

"Oh my gosh, Dylan. Do you totally need something?"

I jerked my hand from the door. "Just making sure you're okay in here. Thought I saw a hobo."

Her gaze cut to the lock, my hand, and to my sisters

cowering behind me. "Did y'all come over for some hot chocolate and bedtime stories? Because I totally have some cocoa I can make. Mmm hmmm."

I cleared my throat. I was inches away from backing out of this entire thing. My brilliant plan was foiled. I wanted to do this whole gambit while Dewy wasn't paying attention, wasn't suspecting it.

Sera poked me in the ribs.

What was I thinking? This was a brilliant opportunity. Best I'd ever had. I had Dewy totally conscious and ready to be dinged in the head.

"Actually, there was something I wanted to ask you."

Dewy crossed her arms. "Is it about Colten? I ran into him and he totally asked me out to dinner. You know, the whole seducing thing that I do. I couldn't help it."

I screwed up my memory, focused on the truth spell and said, "No, I didn't want to ask you about him."

"Then what is it you need to know?"

I took one of the steps, tapped my finger to her forehead and said, "Did you attack my family?"

A wave of power rushed up my arm and through my hand. I saw the blue crystallize over Dewy's face. Magic swelled over her like a bubble, fizzing away as quickly as it had been created.

Dewy blinked. She smiled. "Dylan Apel, did you totally just use a truth spell on me?"

Uh-oh. Crap. That wasn't supposed to happen. She was supposed to tell me the truth.

"I have no idea what you're talking about."

"I wish you hadn't done that." Dewy licked her lips. "Really. That was totally a bad idea. I mean, your family has gotten away with a lot of things. A lot. But you're gonna have to pay for this one." A sparkle twinkled in her eye. "For once you're going to face justice."

I swallowed. "What?"

"Yep." Dewy opened her mouth so wide it looked like her jaw unhinged. She paused for a moment, and then she released a high-octave scream.

The sound pierced my body. My knees buckled. My body convulsed. I covered my ears to block the sound as I sank to the ground.

Tears stung my eyes. I blinked, trying to clear the fog in my brain. I had to think of something. Come up with a way out of this. I glanced at my sisters and saw them curled up on the sidewalk same as me. Oh boy, we were in trouble.

Shadows rose from the concrete, appearing from vapors of smoke. My head buzzed. Dewy still screamed. It was difficult to focus, to concentrate on anything.

The figures approached. Dewy's screaming stopped.

"Dylan Apel," one of them said.

"Hello, Em," I croaked.

Esmerelda Pommelton, Queen Witch of the South, glanced down at me. There were three other figures with her. I noticed one was Councilwoman Gladiolas.

"Dylan," Em repeated. She shook her head. "That there witch, Dewy Dewberry, just accused you of usin' a truth serum on her. That true?"

I bit my lip. I didn't know what to say. "Um. I'd like to see my lawyer?"

Em nodded. "You'll get one, chicklet. But right now we've got to take y'all someplace else."

"Where?" I said, my gut twisting.

Gladiolas took a step forward. "Dylan, we're taking you and

your sisters to witch prison."

Em pulled me off the concrete. The other figures grabbed Reid and Sera. Em snapped her fingers and we vanished.

ELEVEN

I sat in a cold, sterile room with my sisters. We'd been kept here for two hours without anyone telling us what was going on.

I was getting hungry. I kinda wanted some cake.

The door smashed open and in walked Roman. He scowled. I cringed. "What's this about?" he growled.

I bit my bottom lip. "I did a spell on Dewy."

He shut the door, grabbed a steel-framed chair and swung it around so its back was facing us. He slid down and sat, crossing his arms on top of it. Ropes of muscle bulged from his neck. I'm thinking Roman was officially PO'd with me.

"They say it was a truth serum spell."

"It was."

He steepled his fingers beneath his chin and sighed. "The penalty for that is prison."

"So I've been told."

"What were you thinking?"

I pulled my knees up under my chin and curled my arms around them. "That she attacked my family. I wanted to know the truth."

Roman's chest inflated as he inhaled. I'm pretty sure he mentally counted to ten to keep himself from snapping. "You can't just go around doing truth serums on people. If crime solving was that easy, there wouldn't be anyone doing crime."

I pulled my legs closer. "Maybe it should be that easy."

He sighed. "What am I going to do with you?"

I smiled cheerfully. "Get me out of this?"

Roman shook his head. "Dewy might press charges."

"She's a unicorn-baby stealer!"

"That doesn't mean she doesn't have rights."

"She's tormenting me. Trying to make me go insane."

"How?" he asked.

"By dating Dylan's ex-boyfriend from high school," Reid chimed.

Roman's gaze flashed over to my sisters. "I can't believe the two of you went along with this."

"Eh. We were bored," Reid said. "But seriously, can you get us out of this?"

Roman shook his head. "Not this time. I don't know any loopholes to free you. Reid, you'll probably be released since you don't have magic."

"Thanks for reminding me," she grumbled.

"Sera, since you didn't actually work any magic, you might also be set free." He leveled his green eyes on me. "But Dylan, I don't know any way for this to be overlooked."

I dropped my feet to the floor. "Dewy's a bad, bad person. Trying to get a little truth out of her shouldn't be a big deal. She tried to seduce you at the Valentine's dance. Doesn't that count for something? Isn't it illegal to try to seduce people with magic?"

"No."

I crossed my arms. "It should be. That's worse than trying to wiggle a little truth out of someone. Especially if your family was just attacked."

"I know it's been stressful, but you have to be patient," Roman said.

"I don't want to be patient. I want to fight. I didn't even get the chance to find out the truth. The spell didn't work."

Roman quirked his brow. "It didn't?"

"No."

He drummed his fingers on the chair. "I'll be right back."

I glance at Reid and Sera. They shrugged. About three seconds later Gladiolas barged in. She wore her normal bland pantsuit. It was gray, the same color as the walls. She fluffed her curly bangs and closed the door.

The councilwoman leaned both hands on the table. "Let me get this straight. You performed a truth serum spell but it didn't work."

I spit out a bit of fingernail I'd been nibbling. "Right. I asked Dewy the question and then she started screaming and you showed up. End of story."

Gladiolas sighed. "Okay. You're released."

My eyes widened with surprise. "We are?"

She nodded. "You didn't actually perform the spell. You didn't get the information out of Dewy, so you didn't work the magic properly. It's a loophole I'm going to exploit for you." She rubbed her forehead. "You girls cause more trouble."

"But we're worth it," I said cheerfully.

"I'm not sure about that," she grumbled. "Gather your things and get out of here before one of the other council members sees you."

I jumped out of the chair and wrapped my arms around Gladiolas. "Thank you."

"You owe me one, Dylan Apel."

"I think I owe you more than one."

We tiptoed from the room and stepped into the dark purple hallway of the witch police headquarters. An eerie feeling crawled over my belly. I stuck my head back inside the room.

"Um, Gladiolas?"

She glanced up. "Yes?"

"We don't know how to get out of here."

"Join hands."

We did.

"Wait." Roman strode down the hall. "Gladiolas, send Sera and Reid home. I'd like Dylan to stay."

"Very well." Gladiolas snapped her fingers, and my sisters vanished.

I turned to Roman. "What's going on? I'm not going to be locked up, am I?" I laughed when I said it, but I knew it might not be too far from the truth.

He hooked his arm around me. "No. There's someone I'm going to take you to meet."

"Who?"

"A contact I've got."

I nodded. "Okay. Why?"

Roman slid his sunglasses down over his eyes. "Because he has information on Edgar Norwood. Information that could help us crack this case."

***

My boots clacked against the black tile of the headquarters. It wasn't that it was gloomy. Okay, it was, with its deep purple walls and black tile flooring. Occasionally a splash of color appeared—a red or teal that kinda made my day—but other than that, it was a dark, ominous place.

Roman held my hand as we walked through the halls. "You're off the hook, darlin'. Why the worried look?"

I shook those thoughts out of my head. "Oh, no reason. Nothing."

He frowned. "Lay it on me."

I scratched the back of my neck. "Why didn't my spell work? I'd performed it before on Reid and had no problems."

Roman shrugged. "I don't know. Could've been a fluke in the spell. Could be Dewy keeps a counterspell cast on herself."

"You think?"

"Maybe. We are talking about someone who tried to kill a baby unicorn."

"Steal its horn," I corrected.

Roman smirked. "Same thing. There's no telling what kind of secrets she's hiding."

We reached the end of the hall and entered a set of glass doors. The vacuum seal sucked as Roman pushed it open. A row of cubicles, now empty given how late it was, lined both sides of the room. A series of glass-encased offices were carved out of the back wall. A light glowed from one.

"That's where we're headed," Roman said.

I clutched his arm as we crossed to it. I swear my feet clacked as loud as gunshots over the floor. Sweat streaked down my back. Yes, I was nervous. To be honest I didn't even know what I was doing here.

Roman knocked on the door.

"Come in."

We entered. A pudgy man with slicked-back gray hair and a balloon for a stomach sat behind a mahogany desk. A cigar rested between two of his meaty fingers. He bit off the end, spat it into the trash and rose, extending his hand.

He spoke with a thick, raspy voice. "Roman, good to see you, my man. Glad you're well."

"Thank you for meeting us."

The man turned to me. "And you must be Dylan."

"I am."

"Smiley Martin at your service."

"Thank you, Mr. Martin."

"Call me Smiley." He grunted. "I heard your time as Queen Witch was very successful."

I laughed. Yes, no wars erupted during my term that lasted about two seconds. "Yeah, I guess you could say that."

The man sat back to his chair and gestured for us to sit. "Don't be modest, kid. You caught two of the bad guys in only a matter of days. Normally I wouldn't be meeting with you, but since you've helped us out, I thought I'd help you out."

He chewed the end of the unlit cigar. "We need to be quick. Security sweeps this level every hour. We've got about twenty minutes before they do so again."

I frowned. "Oh. This isn't your office?"

He shook his head. "No. As far as this whole conversation goes, it never happened. I don't exist to you, and you don't exist to me."

"Got it."

Smiley leaned back in the chair. It squeaked under his weight. "Officially, Edgar Norwood left the witch police years ago. Unofficially, he'd been working on the magic-stealing ring for nearly two decades, trying to edge his way up the ranks."

He paused, glanced toward the hallway. "Everybody down."

We hunkered under the desk for a few seconds. Smiley peeked his head over the lip. "Thought I heard the guard. Guess it was a false alarm. Breaking into an office at night always makes me jumpy."

You think?

We crawled out and resumed our seats. He yanked down the front of his shirt. The material stretched so far away from the buttons that it looked like they were about to pop off and fly across the room. With my luck one of them would hurdle into my eye. But the little round bits of plastic held the shirt together and stayed on. They must've been attached with superglue.

He pulled the cigar from his mouth. "Tell me what happened with Norwood."

Roman explained Edgar's surprise appearance to Boo along with the memory I pulled out of him.

Smiley rubbed his eyes. He sighed, drummed his fingers on the desk. "I'll be honest with you." He paused. "Norwood went rogue. Started out as a good agent, one of the best. Then he got seduced by the magic-stealing side of things and we lost all contact with him. We'd been looking for him for years."

I stopped chewing the inside of my lip. "Is that why he never came out and named who killed Roman's mother and sisters? 'Cause he went bad? From what I saw, he knew who did it."

Smiley nodded. "That's probably a big part of it. Then after twenty years of staying silent, something happens—maybe guilt gets to him and Norwood decides he's going to reveal what he knows, but gets killed before he can do that."

Smiley sighed.

I felt bad for him, felt pain emanating off him. "You were close to Norwood?"

"Before he turned, we were like brothers." He puffed the unlit cigar. "Now he's dead and we don't know who did it. The killer was messy—which is good for us—dumping his body in the gym like that. Listen. I've got an agent in Silver Springs. Someone I want you to work with. Someone who could help you out."

I glanced at Roman. He frowned. "I'm not sure I want to

bring anyone else into this."

Smiley folded his meaty hands. "It's always good to get another opinion on things. We've got someone planted. Listen, I'm sorry I didn't tell you before. Couldn't. Had to make sure it would be safe for them to work with someone else." His gaze slewed from Roman to me. "Now, this person might not be the easiest to work with."

"What's that supposed to mean?" I said. "Do they have a terrible attitude? Or smell bad?"

"If they smelled bad, I'd consider it a blessing," he said.

This didn't sound like it was going to turn out too good.

"The reality is this person doesn't have the best reputation. Used to be on the wrong side of things."

"How far on the wrong side?" Roman said.

Smiley armed a trickle of sweat from his temple. "'Bout as far as you can go without going all the way."

"And how far is that?" Roman said. His jaw clenched.

"Listen, I'm not going to sugarcoat things. You don't have to like the agent, but you have to work together to get this thing solved."

Why did he keep saying the word agent and not the person's name? My stomach pretzeled. I had a bad feeling about this. A very bad feeling.

"Who is this person?" I said.

Smiley bit down on the cigar and cracked his knuckles. "You know, when I first started in this business, I had to partner up with the one guy in the whole department nobody wanted to work with. At first I hated him. Would've rather cut small slices in my arms and poured alcohol on them than work with this guy. That's how much I hated him. But no matter what, I remained professional and got the job done."

"That's great," Roman said. "Makes my heart bleed for you.

A name."

"I want you to keep an open mind."

"Who is it?" I hissed.

As soon as he opened his mouth, I knew exactly what Smiley was going to say. He didn't even have to say the name. I knew what evilness was going to come out of his mouth. As soon as he puckered up his lips, I cut him off.

"Don't tell me—"

He thumbed his nose. "Agent Dewy Dewberry."

I threw up in my mouth.

TWELVE

"Dylan, you have to get up. You can't stay in bed all day."

"Pretty sure I can."

Sera yanked the comforter off me. She thumped my forehead.

"Ouch."

"You need to get up."

I pulled the comforter back down and turned over. "I can't. It's too awful."

"What is?"

"Dewy Dewberry is a secret agent for the witch police."

A pause. Then I felt pressure as Sera sat on my bed. "What?"

"She's a good guy, Sera. And now she and Roman will be working together."

"I take it you're worried."

"No," I sniffled. "Of course not. I'm sure she won't try anything awful or terrible or anything like that. I'm sure she'll be a total peach."

"Roman told you not to worry about her."

I rubbed sleep from the corner of my eyes. "I know. He did, but I still don't like her and I don't trust her."

Sera tapped a finger against her bottom lip. "If she's a good guy, why'd she try to get you thrown into witch jail?"

I tossed strings of dirty hair from my face. "I don't know. Why did she do that?"

"You need to find out."

I pushed up off the bed. "I've been so worried about her and Roman working together I didn't even think about that."

Sera handed me a stack of cakes from the side table. "Here. You can take her these while you're at it."

"Did you bake all night?"

She shook her head. "No."

"That's good."

"I did these this morning."

The scent of lemon wafted up my nose. It smelled so good I was tempted to eat a slice for breakfast. "Stop worrying," I said.

"I'm not." She shook her head. "I won't."

"Whatever you say," I said.

I showered, dressed and lugged the cakes with me to Perfect Fit. I paced back and forth, watching Dewy's store the entire time. Finally, I put the BE RIGHT BACK sign up and strode across the street with the confections. I secretly hoped they'd made her gain fifty pounds. That's right, fifty. Why stop at ten?

I knocked on the glass door. Half a second later Dewy answered. The witch was all smiles. She gestured for me to enter.

"Dylan, I totally hope there aren't any hard feelings about me calling the council on you. Mmm hmm."

"No. Of course not," I lied. "In fact, I brought you some cakes to make up for it."

"Thank you," she said sweetly. "Come in and see what I've done with the place."

I stepped into a crisp, white-cubicle-lined heaven. The layout of the boutique was New York chic with white vinyl benches, white cubbies with folded clothes, and gleaming white countertops. Whoa. It was a long way from the other rustic stores on Main Street.

"It's gorgeous," I admitted.

"Thank you."

Before I fell in love with the design and forgot why I was here, I turned to her. "Listen, you and I need to have a talk."

"Sure," Dewy said. "Do you want to piggyback onto my grand opening? You know, run your own specials?"

"No. That's not what I mean. I mean the whole bad-vibe thing going on between us."

Her red lips puckered into an o shape. "I definitely don't want there to be any bad vibes between us. We're totally on the same team here. Even though you always seem to get away with things."

The passive-aggressive tone of her voice sent a jolt of anger through me. "That's what I'm talking about. I might have gotten away with some things, but I've never done anything so bad as steal a baby unicorn."

The air chilled. I swear the room dropped thirty degrees. Dewy stared at me for a long moment before saying, "I paid for my crime. Like totally. You've never paid for anything. In fact, you did a truth serum on me and all you got was a stern talking-to. Not that I wanted you to go to prison, because I totally didn't, at least not for that. If you hadn't been at the jail, then you wouldn't have met Smiley Martin, and if you hadn't met him, you wouldn't know that Roman is supposed to be my partner."

I rubbed my temples. "You had me arrested so that I would know from a reputable source that you're supposed to be partnered up with Roman? That you're witch police?"

She nodded.

Yeah, 'cause that was definitely easier than just telling me.

My head spun from way too much information. "Okay, so why didn't my spell work?"

Dewy leaned close and whispered, "Must've been some magic dust I stole from that baby unicorn's horn."

I gasped. Was she serious? Before I had time to ask, she continued.

"And totally don't worry about Roman." She winked at me with long, fake lashes. "He's in good hands with me. Great hands. Expert hands. When it comes to men, they just can't resist my powers. I'm a seduce-tress—"

"Seductress," I corrected.

I heard the door behind me swing open. I whirled around.

Rick Beck stood in the door. His gaze cut from me to Dewy. From Dewy to me. "Um. Hey, ladies."

A sour taste melted over my mouth. "Hey, Rick. Great to see you," I lied.

Dewy smiled. "Hi, Rick. What can I do for you?"

He rubbed the back of his neck. "Um. Well. I was wondering, Dewy, if you needed any more help in the back. You know, with your shelving or anything."

Right. I'm sure he was talking about shelving. If shelving included getting Dewy naked, then I thought we were much closer to target.

Not that I was judging or anything, and I certainly couldn't read minds, but I could read human and Rick was uncomfortable as heck. And he knew that I knew that he and Reid had broken up. Now I knew the real reason.

Dewy smiled. "Sure, Rick. I've got more work that needs to be done."

I backed toward the door.

"Dylan," she said.

"Hmm?"

"Have a good day."

I let the door slam behind me.

***

When I got home that night, Milly and Grandma were standing outside.

"What are y'all doing?"

Grandma grabbed me by the shoulders. "Dylan. Thank goodness you're here."

"Something about that statement makes me want to walk away as quickly as I can."

"Don't be ridiculous," Grandma said. "You've got perfect timing."

"For what?"

"We've been trying to fix the shields on the house."

I cocked a brow. "Shields?"

Grandma waved her arms. "Yes. You know, the shield that I had installed to keep us safe. The one that no one who wants to harm us can cross."

Right. I was well aware of that shield. It was one of the first spells I ever learned. It was a simple spell that kept folks who wanted to harm you out of your domain or room or house.

Grandma studied the house. "Before the attack I had the shield set just inside the doorway. But now, we're going bigger. I'm extending it to the sidewalk."

"So that it's like a bubble protecting the house?"

"Exactly," Milly said. "A giant bubble no one can get through."

"What if they tunnel underneath?" I said.

My paternal grandmother stroked her chin. "We need to consider that, Hazel. They may send some enchanted dogs to dig tunnels."

Grandma grabbed her head of triangle-shaped hair. "Good grief! What will we do then?"

"How about we start raising cats so they can scratch out their eyes?" I suggested.

"Not a bad idea," Grandma said. "I'll look into that."

I tapped my foot and pursed my lips. "Couldn't we just cast a spell to see who wanted to do us harm? You know, like you taught me ages ago. Focus on who wants to harm us and whoever walks through the door first is the person who attacked."

Milly smiled. "You're learning to be quite the witch. I'd nearly forgotten about that spell."

Pride ballooned in my chest. "Great. Let's do it."

We went inside, my grandmother Hazel mumbling about a herd of cats. I hoped that idea didn't stick in her head. The last thing we needed was a gazillion cats with a gazillion litter boxes that needed changing.

"Dylan," Milly said, "you remember how to work the spell?"

I nodded. "Sure thing."

I focused on whoever wanted to hurt us. Pinpointed my magic and felt the spell swell within me. Magic swooshed outward, enveloping me in a bubble. Half a second later it burst, washing me with fizzy blue magic.

I glanced at Milly. "What happened?"

She shook her head. "Didn't work. Someone's already cast a counterspell cutting us off."

"Great. So there's no way to know who attacked?"

"Not that way, no."

"Okay," I sighed. I felt pretty much done with this day. "I'm going to my room."

I washed my face and sank onto my bed. I pulled out my phone and dialed Roman. No answer. He was probably powwowing with Dewy about who the criminals were.

Great. That wasn't a hit to my ego or anything.

Sera walked in. "Everything okay? I heard you tried to figure out who attacked us with a spell."

"Didn't work. Now Grandma's going to create an army of cats to protect us."

Sera nibbled on a croissant. "Want some?"

"I'm really trying not to stress eat."

"I've turned to stress baking, so stress eating isn't going to be too far away."

I groaned. "I don't need to gain any weight. I may have to run for my life."

Reid popped in. "Why? Someone still trying to kill us?"

"Pretty sure," I said. "Until we figure out who it is."

"I may be able to enlighten this situation," Reggie said.

"You haven't left yet?" I said.

"Oh no. This situation has proved to be most interesting. I'm waiting to see who gets killed first. You or them."

"That's so refreshing," I said. "Thanks for the vote of confidence."

"You're welcome, Just Dylan."

Here we go again. "All right. Tell us what you've got."

"I've been searching some of the other registries, and I've uncovered a secret address for Edgar Norwood."

"No," Sera said.

"How can it be a secret if you found it?"

Reggie flipped its pages to the right. "Because I was very sneaky in my investigation. The home isn't tagged to Norwood specifically. Very difficult to find. I don't believe the witch police know about it, either."

I rose. "So you don't think anyone's been there to search."

"I don't, Just Dylan. I believe you're the only ones who know."

I glanced at my sisters.

"Should you call Roman?" Sera asked.

"I just did. No answer."

Reid nibbled her bottom lip. "Where's the house?"

"In the hamlet known as Double Puddle."

"That's only an hour from here," I said, hopping off the bed.

"Should you try Roman again?" Sera said.

"I'll call him on the way." I picked up my purse. "Y'all coming?"

Sera glanced at Reid. "We're right behind you."

THIRTEEN

We pulled into Edgar Norwood's driveway about an hour later. My headlights illuminated a stone-colored cottage and the wedge of land that lay beyond. A creek cut off to one side, and the trees shot up thick around it. The place was a perfect retreat. In the summer no one would even know anyone lived out here, once leaves covered the branches of the oaks and poplars that abounded.

"How are we going to get in?" Reid said.

I shrugged "You got an idea, Reggie?"

"He might have hidden a key somewhere around the entrance," came the thick, velvet voice. "Or you can slip your hand through the door."

I nodded. "Let's check first, because I'm not feeling the whole stick-my-hand-through-a-wall thing."

The three of us peeked under the pots on the porch.

"Bingo," Sera said, flashing a key. "Now we can get in. But what if there's an alarm?"

"Reggie, I don't know how to spell an alarm."

"I may or may not have an idea about the code," the book said.

"I hope you do."

"Try 1218."

"What's that?" Reid asked.

"His birthday," Book said.

I took the key from Sera and unlocked the door. As soon as I pushed it open, the alarm chirped. I punched in 1218, and it bleeped off.

"Good going, Reg. You saved us scrambling."

"That's what I'm here for, Just Dylan."

Since there weren't any neighbors nearby, I didn't see any reason not to switch on some lights. "Let's see what we've got."

"Looks normal enough," Reid said.

She was right. It looked like a simple country cottage with regular furnishings—couch, table, bookcases. Very tidy. "Let's check the bedroom. If I were him, that's where I'd keep the good stuff."

We ambled toward the back. The bed was neatly made. A thin layer of dust rested on the surfaces. We checked all the basic places—under the bed, the closet, the drawers.

"I don't see anything interesting," Reid said.

"Maybe Roman would have a better idea of where to check," Sera said. "Did you ever get ahold of him?"

"No. He never answered."

Sera gave me a sympathetic look. "I'm sure he'll call as soon as he can."

"Sure. Well, this looks like a complete waste of time. Y'all ready to go?"

Reid shrugged. "I think so."

We headed back to the living room. "I'll tell Roman about this place so he can comb over it and find whatever it was that we didn't."

"Sounds like a plan," Sera said.

The front door opened. I jerked back, instinctively shielding my sisters. No one was there. All I could see was my car and the skeletons of trees surrounding us.

A gray metal ball flew into the room and bounced on the floor.

"What's that?" I said.

The orb settled to a stop. A hatch on top opened with a snick. Smoke flooded from it. A cloud of toxic fumes fogged the air, burning my lungs.

"Everyone out," Sera yelled.

I barged toward the door. A hooded figure appeared, cutting us off.

Well, that's what he thought, anyway. "Oh no you don't," I said.

I gestured toward the ball. It zoomed straight at the figure, hitting him square in the chest.

"Oomph," he said. He raised a hand. A stream of magic zipped into the house. Something shattered behind me.

He coughed and fled from the door. We followed. I held my hand over my mouth. My eyes burned; my lungs ached. Whatever acrid stuff had been in that ball, I hadn't gotten it out of the house soon enough.

I ran into the black, trailing after the attacker. He reached a grove of trees, snapped his fingers and vanished in a plume of streaking smoke.

I stopped, hunched over and coughed up both my lungs. Sera and Reid collapsed on either side of me.

"Reid, your butt's on fire," Sera said between hacks.

"Not again," Reid whined. She wiggled her rear end into a pile of leaves until the sparks subsided.

"You need a new phone." I gagged.

"You need to not put us in danger," Reid countered.

"He must've followed us. Either that or Reggie set us up." I glared at the backpack. "Pull him out."

Reid fished Reggie from her backpack and presented him to me. As soon as my coughing stopped, I crossed to my old sedan and pushed in the cigarette lighter. Yes, it was that old. When it was orange hot, I held it to one of Reggie's edges.

"I swear I will turn you into kindling if you don't tell me the truth. Did you lead that man here?"

Reggie curled back his cover. "No, I most certainly did not. I do not play more than one side. I'm on yours. But I suggest you call someone in case he returns."

I found my phone and called Roman. This time he answered. I told him where to find us and went back inside. The place was a mess. The intruder's magic had shattered a porcelain lamp and ripped up the couch.

"What's this?" Sera said. She lifted a small black box from the floor. It was no bigger than a ring case.

"I don't know." I opened my palm, and she handed it to me. I flipped the lid off the case and found a white marble.

"Do you think this was hidden in the lamp?" I said.

"Must've been. I didn't see it before."

I took it between my thumb and forefinger, lifting it so I could see into the glass. It looked like an ordinary marble, filled with a mass of white swirls.

"Do you think it's important?" Reid said.

"He hid it in the lamp, so it must be."

"But what is it?" Reid said.

"No clue. But it's gotta be important."

Roman rolled onto the driveway about an hour later. Gravel crunched under the tires of his SUV. I felt super useful, what with the marble and all. I couldn't wait to tell him.

The vehicle lurched as Roman shifted into PARK. He killed

the engine and got out. I sped over to him and was about to throw my arms around his waist when the passenger door groaned open.

"I totally hope this doesn't ruin my beauty sleep, what with it being so late and all. Mmm hmm."

I stopped dead. Roman had brought Dewy Dewberry?

"Are you okay?" Roman asked gently.

I shrank. "Fine. We're fine. We were attacked, but it's okay now."

Concern washed over his face. "What are you doing out here?"

"This is Edgar Norwood's house. We were looking for clues."

"Norwood? How did you find it?"

I wasn't sure Dewy knew about Reggie, so I opted not to mention that part. "Um, we did some of our own detectiving."

Dewy walked up, tapped Roman on the shoulder. "I'm totally going inside to start looking."

Roman nodded as she walked away.

Sera rose. "Reid and I will help."

They all exited into the house.

"What happened?"

I told him about the attack. His concern turned into frustration the more I explained.

"You couldn't wait for me?" Roman said. "You could've been killed."

I crossed my arms. "I called you before we came. I called a couple of times. I guess you were too busy with your new partner."

His expression darkened. "I was catching Dewy up to speed."

"Or was she catching you up to speed?"

"What does that mean?"

My heart knew what Titus had told me—that Roman's heart knew Dewy's was tainted. But my brain thought otherwise—Dewy had a habit of screwing with me. She was a self-proclaimed seductress who'd appeared out of nowhere with Colten and she'd gotten me arrested. So all rational thoughts and knowings didn't hold a candle to the twisted knot that Dewy had turned my head into.

"I don't know what it means," I said, defeated. "What are you even doing here with her?"

"She's supposed to be my partner in this, remember?"

"You had Jonathan Pearbottom as a partner before, and I didn't see you riding around with him."

Roman sighed. "You're not giving me a hard time about this, are you? She has useful information."

"Where? In her bra?"

Roman frowned. He rocked back on his heels and stared up into the night sky. "I'm only working with her, Dylan. There's nothing else going on." He stroked my arm. "Don't you trust me?"

I didn't answer.

Roman leveled his gaze on me. "Darlin', you've got to trust me."

"It's not you I don't trust," I hissed. "It's her."

"She's not going to seduce me."

"That's her special power," I screeched.

"Do you know what mine is?" Roman said. "It's being true to those I love."

I shook my head. "I don't know."

Roman tapped his fingers against his hips. "Well, I do know. I can't help you figure this out. This is yours."

I stepped back.

Roman gave me a tight smile. "Sometimes you have to want to trust more than you want to be hurt." He kissed the top of my head and walked past me. "I need to investigate this scene."

He walked inside. I stood in the cold, hugging my arms to my chest. After about twenty minutes everyone came outside.

Roman glanced at me. "We'll come back tomorrow and comb over the place. On first look I don't see anything."

Reid sidled up to me. "What about—"

I stamped her foot. "Ouch!"

"What was that?" Roman said.

"She was going to ask about the man that attacked us? If you found any evidence of him?"

Roman drummed his fingers on the hood of his car. "No. Nothing. But we'll come back tomorrow. Maybe in the daylight we'll find something more substantial."

"All right. Sounds like a plan," I said.

He stared at me. I stared at him. Neither of us made a move to say anything else. Me and my sisters piled into my car and drove away.

"That was weird," Sera said. "Did you and Roman have a fight?"

"Not exactly."

"Then what happened?"

I gripped the steering wheel until my fingers stretched as far as they would go. "I think we just broke up."

FOURTEEN

The next couple of days were a blur. Basically I went through the motions of life, trying to not think about Roman. He hadn't called me, and I hadn't called him. I tried to tell myself that he was busy, but I mean, he could've found ten minutes, right?

By the time the middle of the week hit, I was zombified.

Sera popped her head in my door. "Are you getting up?"

"Do I have to?" I said, still in bed with the covers up to my eyebrows.

"Yes."

"Then I guess I am. What time is it?"

"Six."

I squinted at her. "What are you doing here? You should be at the bakery."

She crossed and sat on my bed. The mattress squeaked under her slight weight. "Reid's watching it. She's only got an evening class tonight. I came to check on you. Make sure you're okay. You haven't said much the past couple of days."

"There hasn't been much to say." I knuckled up to a sitting position. My body felt stiff. "Why can't I move?"

"Because you slept in your jeans."

I sniffed. "That has nothing to do with it."

"Right." Sera threw me a towel. "Go and shower."

I showered and crept into the living room. The scent of cinnamon welcomed me. I peeked my head into the kitchen. Grandma and Nan stood at the stove icing cinnamon rolls.

"So you've decided to join Sera in her own personal bake-off?" I said, eyeing the stack of cakes on the kitchen island. Apparently, she still didn't have control of her emotions. Some people stress eat. My sister stress bakes. Not good for my waistline.

Grandma frowned. "No one's having a bake-off, Dylan."

"Well, they smell and look delicious."

"They should," Grandma said. "It's an old family recipe."

I quirked a brow. "Whose family? Ours? I've never even seen you make those before."

Nan dusted flour from her hands. "My family's recipe. These cinnamon rolls will make you forget all your worries."

I slumped into a chair. "Not even Sera's food can do that."

Sera entered. "Trust me. They can. I tried one. I don't have a care in the world now."

I rolled my eyes. "You didn't have any to begin with."

She nodded. "Seriously. Not one worry. I might actually stop baking so many extra cakes."

"Then why are you sifting flour into a bowl?"

Sera shot me a dark look. "Just keeping my skills sharp."

"Right," I said.

She tsked. "Listen, aside from being attacked by random witches, I have other things to worry about—like making the bakery's rent, keeping Reid employed, and getting plenty of rest and drinking lots of water."

I gestured toward Nan and Grandma. "See? I rest my case. No worries."

Nan plated a roll and slid it across the table. "Try one."

Grandma handed me a mug of coffee. "If you have one care in the world after a bite of that, I'll be a monkey's mother."

I tipped my head. "You're already a monkey king's godmother." That was true. My grandma was, in fact, godmother to Brock the Monkey King. Something she didn't bother to tell us until a few months ago.

"It shouldn't be a far jump, should it?"

"Okay, I'll try it. But what makes you think I have any worries?" All three women shot each other looks. "So Sera told you. It's not a big deal. It was bound to end, right?" I said, meaning Roman. "I mean, nothing lasts forever."

"Sure," Nan said. "Eat now."

So I stopped grumbling and forced myself to take a bite. Cinnamon with a hint of orange slid over my tongue. Icing melted down my throat. I shivered. An immediate calm washed over me. I felt better. Great, actually, as if nothing else mattered. Nothing except this giant cinnamon roll and my mouth.

"Wow," Reid said, popping her head through the door. "These'll make you forget you broke up with your boyfriend."

Sera threw a streak of flour at her. "What are you doing here?"

"Thought I'd get some good food, too. You can't expect me to stay at work by myself."

Sera quirked a brow. "Yes, actually I can. We should be opening soon." She tossed another shot of flour at Reid. It landed squarely on her chest. Reid glanced at the smeared stain.

"This is my best coat," Reid whined. She dashed across the small kitchen, grabbed a handful of flour and tossed it at Sera. It hit her in the face. Sera palmed it off as Reid giggled.

"Gotcha!"

"You little crab apple," Sera said. "I got you in the chest, not the face."

Reid grinned. "Sorry. Fog of war. Makes things get all wonky."

"I'll show you the fog of war." Sera scooped up a handful of flour and aimed at Reid. She threw. Reid ducked. The flour sailed through the kitchen, landing on my shirt.

"Hey. I don't want any part of this. Y'all's fight has nothing to do with me."

"Oops," Sera said. "You're a casualty."

"Yeah, Dylan," Reid said. "A casualty."

Sera scooped up some more and tossed it at me. It landed in my hair.

I rose. "Hey."

Both of them laughed. If war was what they wanted, that's what I'd give them. I raced to the counter, grabbed two handfuls of flour and threw it at both their faces.

"Hey," Reid said.

"Stop," Sera said.

"Fog of war, ladies. You're both casualties in the great flour battle."

Grandma fluffed her hair. "This isn't the Great Flour Battle. That occurred in the sixties during the Witch War. A herd of witches got into a baking factory. That's when another cluster of witches met up with them. It was a messy, messy battle from what I understand. No casualties, which is remarkable."

A glob of flour landed on her head. Grandma glanced at Reid and Sera, who both stood looking totally innocent. They were pointing to each other, each one placing the blame on the other sister.

"It wasn't me," Reid said.

"Not me," Sera said.

Grandma smirked. She lifted her hands, and the bag of flour

rose from the counter. It sailed over her head straight for Sera and Reid, where it ceremoniously dumped half its contents on both of them in the blink of an eye.

Both my sisters stood covered in white from head to toe. They stared at Grandma. I started to laugh. They looked at each other. Next thing I knew all the extra flour on their arms was being rubbed on me.

"Hey," I said.

"Sorry," Reid said, "the confusion of war and all that."

When they stopped, I glanced down at the fine dust covering me. I looked at Reid and Sera and we all burst into laughter.

"We'd better get cleaned up," Sera said. "My doors should open in ten minutes."

I let them go on ahead of me for the showers. I finished eating my cinnamon roll and washed it down with another cup of coffee.

"So what about your problems?" Nan said. "All gone?"

I drained my cup and set it down with a thud. I felt kinda warm and fuzzy inside as if yes, all my problems were gone. I didn't have anything to bother me at all.

Had something been bothering me? I cleaned up my plate, took a shower and got ready to face the day. My heart felt full. By the time I was ready to head out, it was nine o'clock. Perfect. Right on time.

I slapped on some pink lip gloss and draped a scarf around my neck. Someone knocked on the front door. I heard Grandma go over to answer it. I shouldered my purse and headed for the kitchen, thinking I'd go out the back.

"Dylan," Grandma called. "Are you still here?"

I toward the living room. "Yeah, I'm here."

She pulled me aside. "There's someone at the door for you."

I raised a brow. "Oh? Who is it?"

"It's the agent. I think she said her name was Dewy Dewbetty."

"That's Dewberry."

"Yes, that's the one. She's here."

My good mood deflated. All the worries and butterflies in my stomach returned.

Great. I reached the front door and found Dewy waiting for me. "Hey, Dewy. What's going on?"

Her big blue eyes were all deer-in-headlights wide open. "Yeah, mmm hmm. Well, it's about the other night."

"What about it?"

"Yeah, well. My boss wants to talk to you."

"Okay. I'll be at my store at ten."

"Yeah. Mmm hmm. So that's where you'll be?"

"Where's Roman?"

She cleared her throat. It kinda sounded like Snow White calling birds and creatures to her. I wouldn't have been surprised if a herd of tiny animals showed up to help Dewy do something—like exist.

"Yeah, well, Roman is totally busy and stuff."

"I guess you're keeping him that way."

She smirked. "Trying to. So far that man stays occupied." It was more of a grumble than a brag.

Fist pump for me! She hadn't managed to corrupt him yet. Not that it mattered. "Tell your boss to come to my store. I'll see him there."

"Okay, great. I'll tell him."

An hour later I was waiting for my first customer at Perfect Fit when in walked Smiley with Dewy trailing him.

This time he wasn't chewing on a cigar. Instead he was flipping a nickel between his fingers.

"Good to see you, Dylan. Good to see you. So this is your

place, huh? Where you earn your keep?"

"That's right. I have a small line of men's clothing if you'd like to try on a shirt."

He glanced around the store. That nickel worked its way down his knuckles and back up. "Yeah, I'll take a new shirt. You can put one in the mail for me. Dewy'll give you the address."

I guess it would be complimentary since he didn't offer his credit card? "Sure. I'll get right on that." I paused, waited for him to tell me what was going on. I looked from him to Dewy. "Couldn't find Roman?"

"He's busy, Dylan. Busy man out there trying to find criminals, which is what I hear you've been doing."

"You mean the other night."

"You did us a real favor. A huge one by finding Norwood's secret house. I owe you for that. Big deal. Huge deal."

"Thank you," I said.

"I understand you and your sisters were there for an hour before my people arrived," he said.

"That's right."

He stroked his thumb down his swelling stomach. "Funny thing, really. I was wondering if while you were there alone, you happened to see or find anything different."

I quirked a brow. "Different?"

"Interesting. You know. Out of the ordinary." His eyes rolled around my store. "Like the stuff you have in here." He crossed over to a dress and pawed at the material. "Different. Unique."

Did they know something or were they just guessing? I tapped a finger to my cheek. "Let me think about that."

"Yeah, think about it."

I shook my head. "Nothing comes to mind. I didn't see anything interesting."

"Dewy tells me a lamp was broken in the attack."

"Sure was."

"Some might say that's interesting," he said.

Dewy glanced up from the row of dresses she was picking through. "Mmm hmm. Yeah. That was different."

What were these two? The bobbing-head twins? "The lamp got broken. That's was the only interesting thing that happened."

Knuckling Nickel Smiley Martin flashed Dewy a look. "If you say there wasn't anything interesting, then there wasn't. Sorry to bother you."

I nodded. "It's no bother. You can stop by anytime."

They left. Good riddance. I palmed my pocket, remembering the marble I'd stuck in my jeans. How could I have forgotten about it? Oh, that's right. I'd been wallowing in a little bit of sorrow over my fight with Roman. I was just lucky my diet hadn't consisted of nothing but hot fudge sundaes for every meal.

My fingers slid over smooth fabric. Crap. Where had I left those jeans? I racked my brain. I'd thrown them in the hamper, where they'd sat the past couple of days.

But today was laundry day. Today Nan would empty all the hampers and wash everything.

Would that be bad? I mean, it was only a marble. Surely you couldn't destroy it. But what if you could? What if the thing was magic and submerging it in detergent hurt it some way?

An uneasy feeling crawled over my stomach. I chewed my fingernails. Deciding action was better than no action, I picked up the phone.

"Hello," Milly said.

"Hey, Milly."

"What's going on, toots?"

"Nothing other than I just got a creepy visit from some high-up guy in the witch police."

"Oh? What'd he want? Your soul?"

"Ha-ha. No. At least I don't think so." I considered that possibility. "Actually, he might have and I just didn't realize it."

"Watch those bureaucrats. They're always no good."

I drummed my fingers on the desk. "Thanks for the advice. Listen, that's not why I'm calling. I found something at Edgar Norwood's house."

"What?"

"It looks like a marble and was hidden inside a box that was inside a lamp. I think Nan might wash it today. Would that be bad?"

"Depends on what it is. If the magic inside is sensitive, all that abrasive soap could rub it right off. Or the water could clog the thing's brain. Does she have to wash it?"

"No, she'd be doing it by accident."

"Dylan, that marble might be the key to figuring out who killed him and who's after you. Get it back."

"Okay, thanks." I hung up and called the house. No answer. My grandmother had a bad habit of ignoring the phone, and during the day Nan often wore her headphones so she could tune the world out. It wasn't even classical music. She listened to head-banging kind to stuff. So Nan could be ready to fight at any time, she said.

Yes, I live with a bunch of wackos. I looked at my watch. The store would open in five minutes. I grabbed my bag and rushed over to Sera's.

"Hey, can Reid watch the store until I get back?"

Sera bagged a chocolate chip muffin and rang up Mrs. Allen, a nice older lady with a huge sweet tooth.

"Hey, Dylan," she said sweetly. "I see you're getting a little competition across the street."

"Yes, ma'am. Looks like it. But I'll still have clothes that you like to buy."

"You got in any more of those candles I like?"

"No, ma'am. Christmas wiped me out. Should be getting another shipment in the next two weeks."

Mrs. Allen stared at me with beady eyes. "I hope so, because I hate to have to find another place to shop."

"Me too." Sheesh. What is wrong with people? They were just some freakin' candles. I'd have them in soon.

She left, so I repeated my request since my sister hadn't responded. "Sera, can Reid watch the shop for a few minutes? I have to run home."

"That's fine. What's up?"

"I'm afraid Nan's going to wash all the magic out of that marble."

Her face paled. "The one from the other night?"

"Yeah."

"You haven't done anything about it?"

I shook my head. "No. I've been depressed, in case you hadn't noticed."

She shooed me toward the door and yelled back, "Reid! Get over to Dylan's and watch it for a few minutes."

I waved. "Thanks."

I headed for the door.

"Oh no!" Reid yelled.

I glanced at Sera, who shot me a confused look.

"Reid," she said hesitantly.

"My pants!"

We both headed for the back. Reid stood in the kitchen, her rear end sparking.

"Oh no," Sera said.

I grabbed a pitcher, dunked it in dishwater and threw it on my baby sister. The spark sizzled out.

"Reid, did you have that stupid phone in your pocket?"

She frowned. "I might have."

"I thought you were going to stop carrying it there," Sera said.

Reid yanked it from her jeans. "But I need it close by."

"You also don't need any skin grafts," I growled.

She rolled her eyes and press the HOME button. "It won't come on."

"That's because I fried its brain. You're just lucky you weren't fried before it was."

Her lower lip trembled. "But my phone."

I grabbed Reid by the arm and pulled her from the kitchen. "Jeez. We'll go get you a new one, okay?"

Her eyes twinkled at that. "Promise?"

"Promise. Now go watch my store. I'll be back."

My heart pounded as I headed for the car. I dialed home again. Still no answer. What was going on? If the phone rang enough, wouldn't my grandmother get annoyed and pick up? And how long could Nan listen to rap and heavy metal? That stuff gave me a headache after five minutes.

"Hey, Dylan, you been inside Dewy's store yet?"

Jenny Butts was walking down Main, heading straight for me.

"Yes, I have."

"It is so cool. That place has some lingerie that I think you couldn't even pass up buying."

I narrowed my eyes. "Now, what exactly is that supposed to mean?"

"Means you might thaw out a little bit."

I shook my head. "Well, at least one of us doesn't need any defrosting. We both know you have a date with a different guy every week. Be careful, Jenny. You might run out of lingerie at that rate. Slow down."

Her jaw dropped. "Why, Dylan Apel, that's the rudest thing—"

"Pretty sure it's no ruder than what you say about my girlie parts every other week."

Jenny cocked her head. "You know, you're probably right."

I opened my car door. "Wouldn't that be a first."

I fired up the engine and rolled down Main. I'd gotten as far as First Baptist Church when a flock of Canadian geese decided to cross the road. For Pete's sake, weren't they supposed to be farther south at this point? I tapped the steering wheel impatiently as they waddled to the other side, heading from one pond to another. I edged the car forward, hoping to speed them up, but it had no effect.

When the last one slipped past my bumper, I hauled rear end down the street. Flashing lights in my rearview caught my attention. Where had the cop come from? I groaned as I threaded onto the shoulder.

Officer I've-got-nothing-better-to-do Howie strolled up to my window. "Hey, Steve," I said.

"Hey, Dylan," he said, tipping his hat. "You all right?"

"Yep, sure am. Just trying to get home."

He whistled through the gap in his front teeth. "You sure are. Doing fifty in a thirty."

"Yeah, I'm really sorry about that, but Grandma isn't answering the phone. She always answers. I'm worried that she might've had a stroke or something."

Steve's brown eyes widened. "Seriously?"

I nodded. "At her last doctor's visit he said she was at risk. Ever since, I've been really worried about her. She usually answers the phone, but she didn't."

"Gosh. You think she's had a stroke?"

I gnawed the inside of my cheek. "I think it's possible."

It was possible, though not likely. But in all honesty, I didn't need a ticket right now. Let's face it—I didn't need a ticket ever.

Steve stepped back. "You need an escort?"

I shook my head. "No, I'm okay. I just have to get home."

He wagged a finger at me. "Go on. But take it easy down Main. I don't need anybody getting run over."

"Sorry. I'll go slower."

I rolled off and took a right on Spring. I kept my eyes open, waiting for something else to stop me in my tracks. I mean sheesh, how was I ever supposed to get home with all these interruptions?

I slid into a space next to the curb and killed the engine. When I entered the house, I found Grandma sitting on the couch watching As the World Turns or some other soap opera.

She shot up and quickly flipped off the television. "Dylan, is everything okay?"

"Where's Nan?"

Grandma shrugged. "She's around and about. I'm not her keeper, Dylan. I don't have a radio collar on her so I can track her every movements. But that does remind me of the time we were tracking a unicorn killer. I knew the only way to stop him was for me to go undercover as one of them."

I really needed to find Nan, but this was too good to pass up. "So you dressed up as a unicorn?"

Grandma adjusted the scarf wound around her neck. "Of course. What else was I going to do?"

"Got me there."

"So I dressed up like a unicorn. I had a tracking collar clamped to my leg so in case I was stolen by the witch, the other police would be able to find me."

"And? Did you get stolen?"

"No."

"Shocker."

I left for the laundry room. "Nan! Nan!"

No answer. I pushed open the door and sighed. There she stood, headphones on and music blaring.

"Nan," I said.

She switched the music off. "Yes?" she screamed.

"Have you washed my clothes?"

"Yep! They're all done. I fought a nasty ketchup stain on your sweatpants, but I won. I always do."

My gaze shifted to the laundry basket. Sitting on top were the jeans I was looking for. My hopes sank. "You washed my jeans?"

"Fresh and clean," she said, handing them to me.

I felt the pockets. They were empty. "Did you see a box in them?"

She nodded. "Sure did."

I grabbed her by the shoulders. "Where is it?"

"On your dresser."

I kissed her cheek and ran to my room. The box was exactly where she said. I opened it. The marble sat intact. I fished my phone from my purse and dialed Milly.

"I've got the marble."

"Get over here. Let's see what it is."

FIFTEEN

I grabbed Grandma and drove over to Milly's. She greeted us with her usual cheery composition.

"My bursitis is acting up again. We need to make this snappy."

"Well hello to you too," I said, stepping inside.

"It makes me grumpy when it flares," she explained.

I smacked my lips. "And that's different how?"

"Watch it, toots," she said.

Grandma and I entered the living room. Polly Parrot screeched from his gilded cage while the boa constrictor flashed its tongue from the aquarium sitting beside it.

"Looks like you're still traumatizing Polly. I'm pretty sure PETA would have a field day with this."

Milly grazed her finger over Polly's head. "Shows how much you know. These two are becoming friends."

I quirked a brow. "They are?"

"Teddy tried to eat Polly. Once he realized his prey was a wooden bird, he laid off."

"Teddy, huh? Snuggly as a bear?"

Milly grunted.

"Anyway, smart snake," I said. "Listen, I've got to get back to the shop. Here's the marble."

I handed the smooth stone to her. Grandma peered over Milly's shoulder.

"Looks like a balding stone," Grandma said.

"I'd have to agree," Milly said.

"What's a balding stone?"

Grandma clapped her hands with something akin to glee, which I didn't understand a bit of. "It's a stone used to hold certain types of information. Could be memories, could be ideas a person's had." She slid a finger lined with age over the surface. "They used to be very popular up until a few years ago. Now everyone stores information in the cloud."

I smirked. "You mean like the Internet cloud?"

Grandma shook her head. "No. An actual cloud. There's a pink one made of magic that has limitless storage for data. Magical data. It sits to the North of us."

"Of course it does." Because everything in the witching world always made a thousand pounds of sense. "So what about this balding stone?"

Milly palmed it. "To use it, you need the balding device."

I sank back onto the couch. "What's that?"

"It's a cushion that the stone sits in. It's a magical construct. The designer of the cushion stopped selling them years ago when they went out of fashion."

I tipped my head back and stared at the ceiling. "So can we get one?"

"I'm not sure," Milly said.

"Why's that?"

"The designer's dead."

Well that would explain it. "Maybe there's still some around. Who would know?"

Milly and Grandma exchanged glances.

"What?" I said. "What am I missing?"

Grandma tilted her head back and forth. "His daughter is still alive."

"That's good. She might be able to help us. Who is it?"

Milly grinned. "Queen Em."

My hopes crashed and burned on the tarmac. "Seriously? Does he have another daughter? One I might get along with?"

It wasn't that I didn't like Esmerelda Pommelton. It was more we didn't see eye to eye on things. I exhaled. "Okay. It looks like I need to track Em down. Anyone know where to find her?"

Grandma stared at me as if I'd grown five heads. "At Castle Witch. Where else?"

Right. I was hoping the answer was going to be somewhere else, but it looked like I was wrong. "Okay. Y'all coming with me?"

Milly and Grandma both shook their heads. "You'll go this one alone, toots. I'll transport you there."

"Good," I said. "So I won't have to hear about missing hands and feet from Grandma. She always says that whenever she sends me anywhere."

Milly laughed. "I'll make sure to get your head and feet where we're going. It's your body I'm worried about."

I gulped down a knot in my throat. "Don't you both want to see what the marble tells us?"

"Yeah. Bring the device back here."

"Okay, will do. Now send me to the castle."

Milly grinned, raised her hand and snapped her fingers. In a flash of light, she and my grandmother vanished.

***

Milly had planted me right in front of the main doors leading into the castle. I took a deep breath and walked inside. I found a servant and told him I needed to see Em. I waited in the solar until she arrived.

The room was circular with sky-high windows. Light sliced through glass, practically making the room sparkle.

"Dylan Apel, the trouble meter inside my head didn't go off when you arrived. You must be toein' a straight line today."

"Ha-ha. I haven't gotten in trouble in…days."

Em flipped a cascade of cinnamon and crimson curls over her shoulder. "You'll probably be back in trouble tomorrow."

"Thanks for the vote of confidence."

Her coral-colored lips coiled into a smile. "You're mostly welcome."

"Listen, Em, as great as it is to catch up, I need some help."

She waved her hand, and a service of hot chocolate appeared. Em flew a cup over to me. "From little ole me? What can Queen Witch do for y'all?"

"I need to find a balding device."

Her eyebrows shot up to the ceiling. "Why would you need one of those?"

"Because I want to take a picture of it for posterity."

She stared at me blankly.

"Em, I have a balding stone. I need the device to read it."

The queen frowned. "Who's balding stone?"

"Not sure I'm going to tell you that."

She set her mug on the table and rubbed one bone-colored hand over the other. "I ain't got one."

"Do you know who does?"

She nodded. "My father taught one other person the secrets of the stone."

"But he didn't teach you."

She shook her head. "He knew the technology was temporary. I don't think he wanted it to be that way, but witches are always coming up with new ways to do things—new spells, potions, you name it. So I never bothered to ask, and he didn't bother letting me know."

"But someone knows."

She nodded. "Yes, one other person."

I scooted to the edge of my seat. "Well, who is it? Who knows it?"

Em smirked. "Why should I tell you? Seems like I should be tellin' that boyfriend of yours. You know, the one who's supposed to be doin' all the investigatin'."

I rolled my eyes. "Come on, Em. We've been through a lot together. Don't you owe me one?"

She tapped a foot on the marble floor. "Seems like I might owe somethin'." The queen rose. "Come on. I'll take you to him."

Em led me through the castle to the village that sat behind it. We wove through the cottages until we reached the very last one. I stopped, confused.

"Em, this is Roman's house. What are we doing here?"

Her green eyes sparkled as she said, "You'll be seein'."

She knocked. The door swung open. I stepped back, half expecting to see Roman and not feeling quite up to it, if you wanted to know the truth. But instead of Roman, Boo answered the door.

"Em, Dylan. Good to see you. Come on in."

"Boo, what are you doing here?" I asked.

He shuffled over to the stove, where it looked like he was cooking up a grilled cheese sandwich. "Well, Dylan," he said in that slow drawl of his. "Roman thought it'd be better if I stayed at the cottage for a while. He spent the last couple of days transitioning me here." He flipped the sandwich over. "You know, just in case. Can't be too careful."

So that's what Roman had been doing. Maybe that's why he hadn't called. "I'm glad you're safe."

"Castle Witch has some of the best defenses in all the witch kingdom," Em said.

Boo turned away from us to plate his sandwich.

I frowned. "Okay," I whispered to Em. "Where's the person we're supposed to meet? Who knows about the stone?"

Em ignored me. "Richard," she said, "Dylan needs a favor from you."

Boo's eyes lit. "I'd be happy to oblige. Anything I can do to help, you all know that." He settled into a wooden chair. "It's hard coming back and feeling like my talents aren't being used."

Em sat next to him. "That's what we need. Your talents."

He bit into the crisp sandwich and chewed for a minute. "And which talents might those be?"

Em smiled. "We need you to read a balding stone for us."

Boo's hand slid over his beard. "Em, you know it's been a long time since I've tinkered with one of those."

She nodded. "I know, but you know my pop wasn't gonna be trustin' any old turd ball."

I grimaced. Nice image.

"Do you have a device?" he asked Em.

"There's one in the castle museum."

His gaze cut to me. "And you've got a stone, I take it."

I nodded. "It belonged to Edgar Norwood."

His mouth opened at that. Richard shoved the rest of the sandwich in his mouth. He slapped his thigh. "The heck we doing sitting around here? Let's go read the stone."

SIXTEEN

We got the device from the museum and returned to the cottage. I handed Boo the stone. He rubbed his palms together. I wasn't sure if he was warming them up or readying for the task ahead.

"Now. Let's see if this works." He pulled a screwdriver from his pocket and made a few adjustments to the device. Milly and Grandma had explained the thing exactly. It looked like a velvet cushion pressed snug into a wooden box. The box itself had switches and wires and screws, which was what Boo was fiddling with.

"Okay, let's try this." He placed the marble in the center of the cushion. I crossed my fingers, hoping that in about five seconds we would know who the killer was. Or at least some sort of information that would make my life easier.

"Doggonit, why didn't it work?" Boo said, scratching his head. He tinkered with the box some more and replaced the marble. Once again I crossed my fingers. Still nothing.

"The marble's encoded," he said.

"You mean like with magic?" I said.

He nodded. "You'll have to break the code to get it to work

in the device."

I chewed the tips of my fingers. "Em, you have any ideas on this?"

"I ain't got one notion, chicklet. You'll have to take this to Milly and Hazel."

Great. "Is that okay with you, Boo? For me to take it?"

"I reckon." He handed the device to me and scratched his forehead. "As far as I know, it should be working. Once you figure out whatever's blocking the marble, it should sing like a whistle for you."

"Awesome. Okay. Well, I'm heading back. Em, can you zip me to my house?"

She frowned. A little crinkle appeared above her nose. It was so cute I wanted to pinch it. Then I remembered Em was a huge redneck and probably wouldn't appreciate that.

She fisted a hand to her hip. "You need to be learnin' how to zip yourself here and there."

"I haven't even been a witch for an entire year, Em. Cut me some slack."

"I'll cut you somethin'," she said.

I wasn't sure what that meant, and I didn't want to ask. "Okay, you ready to send me home?"

The queen snapped her fingers. Next thing I knew, I was standing in Milly's parlor. Grandma was there, too. They were trying to feed that stupid snake some crickets.

Chocolate-covered crickets.

"I don't think he'll eat those," I said.

"Nonsense," Grandma said, fluffing her hair. "Everyone likes chocolate."

"The word 'everyone' refers to people. Not snakes."

Milly and Grandma looked at each other.

"What?" I said.

"Nothing," Milly said. She eyed the balding device. "What'd you find out?"

"That the marble is encrypted. We need to break whatever magic is on it so it'll work. Think y'all can swing that?"

Grandma tugged the strand of pearls around her neck. They were twisted in the gauzy scarf she was also wearing. "Get out of there," she grumbled. The pearls came free. She sighed. "That's better." She glanced at me and smiled. "We can try to fix your marbles."

"There's only one," I said.

"I know, dear, it was a joke about your brain."

"Very funny." I handed her the stone. She ran her fingers over it and mumbled a few words. The marble floated into the air and started spinning.

"We might have something," Grandma whispered.

It spun faster. The streaks inside blurred to a whirl of white. Then it stopped.

I bit my lip, waiting, hoping that in half a second we would have an answer. "Do you think it worked?" I whispered.

"I don't know," Grandma said.

Suddenly a stream of green smoke plumed from the top. Flashbacks of that smoke bomb the intruder threw into Edgar's house lit up my brain.

Milly and Grandma exchanged glances.

"Get out now," Milly screeched.

Grandma pushed me out of the door. Milly followed. As soon as I planted both feet on the porch, Milly slammed the door shut. The house contracted, sucking me backward. I stumbled onto Grandma, who stepped on Milly.

The structure shuddered. The house boomed. I shot a frightened look to Milly.

She shrugged. "Looks like the booby trap on the marble

worked."

Ten minutes later half the witching world showed up. Jonathan Pearbottom, inspector extraordinaire, dipped his parrot-shaped nose into our business.

"Would you like to explain what happened here?"

Grandma wiggled her fingers at him. "A curse gone wrong."

Pearbottom paled. "A curse? Are you cursing someone?"

"Heck's bells, no, Pearbottom. What do you think we are, wicked witches?"

Pearbottom sniffed the air like it smelled of sulfur and farts. "No. Of course not. So what did happen?"

Milly elbowed past Grandma and shoved her way to Pearbottom's face. "A spell gone wrong. No big deal. Happens all the time."

He quirked a brow. "What sort of spell?"

"Something top secret I'm working on for the council. If you want to know, you'll have to ask them."

Pearbottom paled. "That won't be necessary."

"That's what I thought. Now get your goons out of here before the real cops show up and put you to shame."

Pearbottom glared beady eyes of death at her, but he said nothing. Two minutes later he was gone.

"Whew," I said. "Glad he left."

"Milly, why am I getting calls from your neighbors saying you're murdering people?"

I turned to see Roman standing with hands on hips and his lips quirked into a smirk.

"Because I'm a homicidal maniac," Milly said. "Didn't you know?"

Roman propped one leg on a step and leaned on it. "I'm not surprised. But what really happened?"

"Come on in. The air should be clear by now."

The sight of Roman made my heart knock against my chest. Heat flushed my face, and I knew I looked like a hot mess of emotions and hormones. I took a deep breath, told myself this was no big deal and walked inside.

From the way the house had shuddered, I expected the furniture to have overturned and the wall hangings to be lying broken on the floor, but everything was perfectly in place. Even that stupid snake looked fine. Still coiled in its aquarium.

Milly pointed to the floor, where the marble sat. "We were trying to unlock that."

Roman crouched down, giving me a great view of his sculpted cheeks. I nearly fainted.

He picked up the balding stone. "Where on earth did you get this?"

Milly nodded toward me.

I sighed. "In Edgar Norwood's house."

Roman glanced back at me. "Hmm. So I guess it didn't unlock."

"Not exactly," Grandma said. "It tried to poison us with toxic air."

Roman rubbed a hand over his forehead. "You going to try again to unlock it?"

Milly shook her head. "I need something to go on. If we try it again, it'll just do the same thing."

"So I need to know more about Norwood," Roman mused. He slid the marble into his pocket. "Looks like I'm going for a ride." He glanced at me. "Want to come along?"

Before I could stop myself, I whispered, "Sure."

When we reached his car, he opened the door for me. I almost made a snarky remark. You know, the kind whining ex-girlfriends make, but I decided against it. I slid onto the buttery leather, crossed my legs and stared out the window as we rolled through town.

"Were you going to tell me about the marble?" he asked.

The question caught me off guard. I sucked in my breath and said, "I guess so. I mean, no. Probably not."

His jaw twitched, but he didn't say anything.

"Your girlfriend and her boss showed up at my store asking if I'd found anything at Norwood's house."

He frowned. "What girlfriend? You're my girlfriend."

I leaned back and threw him a whatchu-talking-'bout-Willis look. "No. We broke up."

"No, we didn't."

"Yes, we did."

"When?"

"The other night when you didn't answer my calls and you showed up with that seductress on a stick."

Roman chuckled. He placed his left hand at the top of the steering wheel and laid the other on the seat rest between us. "Darlin', if we'd broken up, I think you should've told me."

"I did tell you. I think. Besides, you haven't called me since it happened."

"I've been taking care of some things with my dad."

"You still could've called."

He shrugged. "You needed some time to cool off."

I crossed my arms. "I did not need time to cool anything."

Roman slipped off the road onto the shoulder. The SUV rumbled to a stop. He slid the transmission into park, flipped up his sunglasses and turned to me. He thumbed my cheek and leaned over.

His lips seared my mouth as his tongue slipped over mine. My body ached for him. Who was I kidding? I ached for Roman. I leaned into the kiss. The seat rest cut into my waist, but I didn't care. If there was one thing I enjoyed losing myself in, it was a kiss from Roman.

He pulled back from the kiss and rested his forehead against mine. "Still want to break up?"

"No," I whispered.

"Good. Now let's go."

We got to Norwood's house about an hour later. "So what did Dewy and her boss want?" Roman asked.

"To know if I'd found anything."

"And you didn't tell them."

"No. I don't like her. So I took the marble to Milly and found out that it was a balding stone and I needed a balding device. So I tracked that down with the help of your father."

He raised an interested brow. "You went to Castle Witch."

"Yeah."

"You hate that place," Roman said.

I shrugged. "It's not so bad. Anyway, what are we looking for? Haven't you already combed over this place?"

He pushed the door open. "I'm looking for anything that will help us crack that marble. Anything strange looking."

There was nothing out of the ordinary about the house. It looked like your run-of-the-mill country home. "When I find a three-pronged fork, I'll let you know."

Roman smiled. He grazed his fingers down my hand. My skin sizzled under his touch. He paused, threw me a seductive glance. "We could try the bedroom first."

Nerves the size of dragonflies buzzed in my stomach. "Ha-ha. Very funny. I'm going to stick to the kitchen."

"Your loss," he said, walking off.

I opened all the drawers and cabinets. Nothing looked strange. Of course it didn't help that I had no idea what I was looking for.

Roman entered a few minutes later. "Find anything?"

I shook my head. "No. Did you?"

He nodded. "Found a book on animal familiars."

I shrugged. "How's that important?"

He slid it across the counter. "Open it."

I peeled back the dark blue cover to the first page. On it was a hand-written note. "Edgar, when you feel the end is near, find me." —Professor Alias.

"Professor Alias?" I said. "Who's that?"

Roman shook his head. "I don't know, but I know someone who does."

"Who?"

"Reggie. Where is it?"

I smacked my lips. "I think Reid has it."

"Then we need to find Reid."

I called Reid, who was still holding down the fort at my store.

"Reggie's back at the house," she said. "You can call my cell number now; Grandma bought me a new phone."

"Oh, she did?"

"Yeah, she just brought it to me. Exact same phone but hopefully it won't set fire like the last one."

"Fingers crossed," I said. After hanging up, I turned to Roman. "Reggie's at the house," I said. "Let's roll."

We headed back into town. He played some rock on the radio. I kicked my feet up to the dash and leaned back, basking in the sunshine as it filtered through the windows.

"Don't scuff up the dash."

I inspected the plastic. "Too late," I said. "It's gonna need a buff job."

"I know someone else who's going to need a buff job."

I squinted at him. "Was that supposed to be suggestive of something between the sheets?"

"Yes?" he said.

"It sounded more like something one lizard does to another."

He smirked. "You'd never know you were related to your grandmother."

I bolted up. "Hey. What's that supposed to mean?"

"I'll give you three guesses. First two don't count."

I rolled the back of my tongue in annoyance. "Whatever."

We reached the house and went inside. Grandma had changed into a pink housecoat and furry bunny slippers. "You're just in time. I made sausage balls for lunch."

"Yeah, I'm not sure I'm in the mood for party food right now," I said.

"Dylan, sausage balls are like manna from heaven. You may not know this, but there was a time I lived on dried sausage balls for weeks."

"When was that?" Roman asked.

She wiggled her fingers. "When the fairies in Fairyland were capturing witches and tickling magical secrets out of them."

I nodded. "Tickling them, huh?"

Grandma leaned in as if sharing a super confidential tidbit of information. "Tickling is the best torture ever invented. You'll get what you want out of someone faster by tickling them than by torture."

"You don't say," I said.

"I do say." She shoved a tray under my nose. "Now. Why don't you try one?"

So we ate a late lunch comprised of sausage balls and lime sherbet punch. Nan had made the punch. When the sugar coma trying to overtake me had me unhooking my belt and looking for my bed, Roman nudged me.

"Where's Reggie?"

"Oh right." I led him to Reid's room. I found her backpack easily enough and dug through it. "Huh. It's not here."

"Do you think it could be anywhere else?" Roman said.

I shrugged. "No clue. Hey, Reggie, where are you?"

No answer. I called Reid again.

"It's there. In my backpack. That's the last place I put him."

"He's not here now," I said.

"Then I don't know where he is," Reid said.

I groaned. "Great."

I hung up the phone and turned to Roman. "It's supposed to be here."

He left the room and headed toward the kitchen. I followed him quick as lightning. We found Nan and Grandma washing dishes.

"Has anyone been here? In the house?" he asked them.

My grandmother paused. "No one except for that nice electrician man who came to check out the ceiling fan."

"Grandma, no one called an electrician," I said.

She shrugged. "He said someone did."

I smacked my forehead. "What did he look like?"

Nan licked her lips. "Well, he wasn't showing any butt crack, so I thought he was handsome."

I rolled my eyes.

"Anything else you remember about him?"

Grandma shook her head. "No he was a pretty regular looking handyman."

"Do you know what company he came from?" I asked.

Grandma pursed her lips. "Hmmm. No."

"Did you write him a check?"

She shook her head. "Said he didn't need payment."

"Figures," I said. I turned to Roman. "I'll see if Milly can perform a magical tracking spell to find the book."

Roman nodded. "Sounds like a plan. You want to call and ask her that?"

I spit out a bit of hangnail. "No. I'm kinda afraid she'll kill me when she finds out. I'll wait."

He glanced at Grandma. "Ever heard of a Professor Alias?"

She clutched the pearls around her neck. "Professor Alias! I haven't heard that name in a long time." She fluffed her hair. "Is he nearby?"

"I don't know," I said. "Why?"

She opened her eyes wide like that stupid Dewy Dewberry always did and said, "If you see him, tell him I said hello."

"I would if I knew where to find him."

"He's probably still working at the university."

I frowned. "What university?"

She pressed a finger to her lips to suggest silence. "Auburn University, of course. In the science department."

Roman scrubbed a palm down the two-day-old stubble on his chin. "Will he go by Alias?"

She nodded. "I believe so."

***

Alias did, in fact, go by Alias, and he was open to meeting us the next day, which required more time spent in the car than I was looking forward to, but hey, you gotta do what you gotta do. Reid was nice enough to watch Perfect Fit as the only class she had was online.

We found Alias in an annexed building at the university. Some ancient structure that used to be part of the science department but was abandoned by the rest of the staff when the new building was erected. Apparently Alias decided to stay.

As soon as I stepped inside, I understood why.

The main laboratory resembled a hothouse more than a lab. Small trees and birds filled the nooks and crannies of the space.

Several tables sat in the middle, and those were filled with bubbling beakers, distilled liquid in vials, colorful solutions—it was sort of a mad scientist's dream come true.

"Alias," Roman said. A man at the very end of the room whirled around. He wore a white lab coat and held a piece of chalk in one hand. He'd been scribbling on an old-fashioned chalkboard.

Untamed gray hair nested his head, and round glasses perched on his nose. His movements were quick, birdlike. He was, all in all, a rather strange little man. I could see why my grandma liked him. "Yes, yes, that's me. Alias. Who wants to know?"

"We spoke on the phone," Roman said.

Alias grasped his hands behind his back. "Yes, yes. What can I help you with?"

"I understand you knew Edgar Norwood."

He clipped his head from side to side. "Norwood? No, I don't think I'm aware of that name."

I pulled out the book on animal familiars and tapped the inscription. "You signed this here."

He stared at the page and then cut his gaze from me to Roman and back to the page. "Interesting that someone would forge my signature. But I'm sorry to say I don't know him."

"Norwood was murdered a few days ago," Roman said.

Alias shuddered. "Terrible. The things people do to one another. But I'm sorry to say, I still don't know him."

I glanced at Roman. He sauntered up to one of the wooden tables and tapped his fingers. "Hazel Horton says hello."

Alias froze. I swear his eyebrows rose three feet. "H-h-h-azel? How do you know her?"

Roman pointed at me. "That's her granddaughter."

Alias stared over the rim of his glasses at me. He came close, grabbed my ears and turned my head from side to side. "Yes, I see the resemblance. It's faint, but it's there." He sighed. A dreamy expression splashed across his face. "Hazel. How is she?"

I pulled from his grasp. "First, tell us about that message to Norwood."

Alias pulled up a stool and sat. "I'm not a witch by nature, but I've worked in potions all my life, trying to help witches solve problems. Warts for instance. Some witches have terrible luck with that. I've created potions to get rid of them. It's been my life's work to help others."

I tapped the book where he'd signed it. "What does this mean, though? When you feel the end is near, find me."

Alias pulled off his glasses and polished them. "You know that some witches have familiars. Or at least they used to. It's not as common a practice anymore, though there are certain things familiars do that are useful."

"Like what?" I asked.

"They can channel magic, help you find objects, that sort of thing." He held up his hand and a yellow parakeet landed on the tip of his finger. He watched as the bird preened its feathers. "Have you ever wondered how familiars are created?"

"No," I said. "Not once."

"It's the soul of a person inside the body of an animal. When the person is about to die, they work a bit of transmutation magic. The theory is that when death comes, their soul will then be whisked out of the body and channeled into a new one."

"An animal's," Roman said.

"Right."

"And you were teaching Edgar about this?" I said.

Alias nodded. "It's the cornerstone of my research. Not what the university knows about, of course. It's a secret. But something I'm passionate about. Edgar knew how to do the transmutation."

"And now he's dead," I said.

Alias leaned forward. His eyes sparkled. "Is he?" he said.

I smoothed the crease forming in my brow. "What are you saying? Do you mean Norwood's somehow alive?"

Alias lifted his hand, and the bird flittered away. "Yes and no. If Norwood followed the spell, then at the time of death he transmuted into another form."

"You mean he's a familiar."

Alias smiled. "Exactly. Norwood may currently be inside the body of an animal. If you want to know his secrets, there's one thing you must do."

I nodded. "We need to find him."

SEVENTEEN

We stayed and talked to Alias for a while and then took our time getting home, stopping to eat supper on the way back. By the time we returned, it was so late I wouldn't be getting much beauty sleep.

Reid was still up, sitting in the living room. She was hugging a pillow so hard I thought she might start making out with it.

Kidding.

"Are you okay?" I asked.

She sniffled. "As okay as I'm going to be."

I wrapped my arms around her. "Is it Rick?"

She nodded. "I just don't understand why he did it. Why'd he break up with me? And why does he live next door? Now I have to look at him every day."

I squeezed her shoulder. "Only if you spy on him with the binoculars. It's not mandatory that you make sure you run into him all the time."

"Very funny. But, it hurts."

I sighed. "I'm sorry. I know it does. There's nothing I can say that will make that pain go away." I tapped her thigh. "Scootch." Reid shifted over and I sat down. "You were doing good a couple of days ago. What happened?"

Reid shrugged. "I don't know. I guess I started thinking about it. It's just— This is going to sound stupid."

I threaded my fingers through her hair. Reid sighed. She shifted, lying down, and pressed her head into my lap. She used to do that all the time when she was a little girl, but since she'd grown up, Reid had become too big for that sort of sister/sister bonding.

I started braiding her hair. "Nothing you say is going to sound stupid."

"I wish I had what you and Roman have."

I choked back a laugh. "Reid, my relationship isn't perfect. It's far from it. The other day we got into an argument and I thought we'd broken up. Roman didn't see it that way at all. He just thought I needed a little air in my sails, I guess. Some time on my own to think."

"What's there to think about? He loves you. You love him."

"It's more complicated than that."

"Only because you make it."

I tugged her hair. "I thought I was the one giving out advice."

"I'm not giving advice, I'm stating fact. You've been worried about this whole Dewy Dewberry situation when you didn't need to be."

"Okay."

Reid sniffled. "Seriously. That woman is nothing more than fluff. Roman knows that. You're the girl with substance. Sometimes you can be a little whiny, but he still loves you, and you love him. Now all you need to do is get married."

"Yeah, right. I don't think that's going to happen any time soon."

Reid sat up. "Why do you fight him so much?"

I shook my head. "I'm not fighting anything."

"Yes, you are. You've fought against this entire relationship from the beginning."

I tucked a strand of hair behind my ear. "Maybe it's this relationship."

Reid frowned. "I don't think so. I think you'd fight any relationship, no matter who it was with. Even Chris Hemsworth."

I gasped. "How dare you speak blasphemy."

Reid giggled. "You don't have to lose yourself in order to love someone. Everyone knows that. And you can't go through life without getting hurt. That's just stupid. But part of living is giving yourself to someone—someone that can hurt you—but trusting that they won't. You can't blame Roman for what Colten did, and you can't let Colten control the rest of your life. Roman deserves more and Colten deserves less."

She paused to scratch her nose. "You have what anyone would want—a good guy who loves you. All you have to do is trust enough to let yourself love him. If you don't, you haven't grown as a person. Heck, what's the point of living on this planet if you don't learn things and become better?"

"Okay, Plato, thanks for the philosophy lesson."

Reid rolled over and patted my head like I was a puppy. "It's not a lesson—it's fact. If you want the relationship with Roman that you deserve, you're going to have to learn how to trust. Yes, that means you might get hurt. Look at me. I trusted Rick and now I'm a sopping mess."

"You're not too bad," I teased.

She flashed me a wobbly smile. "I'm trying. It's just, I thought I loved him. I thought he might have been the one."

"You're only eighteen. You've got a while now before you find the one."

Reid's eyes filled with hope. "You think so?"

"I know so." I gave her a hug and rose. "All right, it's time for you to get some beauty sleep. See you in the morning."

As I walked to my room, I couldn't help but think that Reid was right. I needed to let go of some things—like the past. Roman deserved more, and I deserved more. There was something I needed to do first, though. Something that would set me free. Unfortunately, it would have to wait. I slipped under the covers and slept a dreamless sleep.

***

The next day I knocked on Milly's door bright and early. "I hope you brought breakfast," she said.

"I didn't. I was hoping you'd have biscuits and coffee."

"I've got coffee."

"Great. We're halfway there."

I entered the house and eyed the corner where Polly Parrot and the stupid snake sat perched on a fake branch in its aquarium.

"So what'd you find out?"

"Norwood may or may not have transmuted into the body of a familiar when he died."

Milly poured me a cup of coffee and magicked it over to me. "What else?"

"Please don't kill me," I said.

She snorted. "Great. Bad news. Can't wait to hear what it is."

"You have to promise first. No killing."

She crossed her fingers over her heart. "Let her rip, toots."

I grimaced. "Someone posed as an electrician and stole Reggie."

Milly paused. "That's bad."

"I know! You trusted him with me and he's gone. I'm so sorry."

She shrugged. "We'll get him back. One way or another."

"You think?"

She nodded. "I know."

I released a breath, relieved. "Whew. So. Why would someone steal it?"

Milly caned over to her flowery recliner and sat. "No telling. Maybe they wanted to erase something about themselves or wanted to track down another witch. He holds a lot of information—most of it useful, some of it worthless, but all of it interesting."

"How would someone know where to find it?"

Milly tipped her head from side to side. "No clue. There's the mystery, kid. Lucky for you, since I own Reggie, I know a spell that will get him back."

I drummed my fingers on the couch arm. "What's that?"

Milly smacked her lips. "A retrieval spell. Brings back something you've lost."

"Great. Go ahead and do it."

Milly laughed. "Uh-uh. Since you're the one who lost him, you have to do it."

I sighed. "Okay."

Milly tightened knotted hands over the head of her cane. "Close your eyes and focus on Reggie."

I saucered my cup and set it on a side table. I closed my eyes and settled back in the chair. "Okay."

"Now, in your mind, call out to him. Make the call strong. Make it loud. Become a beacon, lighting the way from wherever Reggie is back to you."

I concentrated all my power. Magic coiled in my belly. It felt like a whirlpool, swirling and twirling in my core. I focused hard. Pressure built behind my eyes and in my head until the coiling mass of magic ballooned outward, popping in a fizzle of power.

I blinked. Opened my eyes. I glanced around the room. "Well?"

Milly shrugged. "It might be in the laundry room."

I rose. Shook my head. "Why would Reggie be there?"

Milly smiled. "Because next to the kitchen it's the best smelling place in the house."

"I'll accept that one from you. You coming?"

She caned over to me. "I'll do even better, toots. I'll lead the way."

I followed Milly to the closet-sized room. She sprang open the door. There, lying on the floor, was Reggie.

"Sweet! You totally called that one." I knelt down and picked it up. Reggie felt light. Very light. Like it was missing half its pages light. "Something's weird."

I peeled back the cover and sank my forehead against the doorjamb.

"What's wrong?" Milly asked.

I sat up and showed her the inside of Reggie.

"Well I'll be," she said.

Exactly. His pages had vanished.

***

Sera sat at the counter of Sinless Confections stirring a mocha. "So why did you need Reggie again?"

"We were trying to track down Professor Alias."

"And now Reggie's interior is gone."

"Stolen," I corrected her.

She shook up a can of homemade whip and added more to

the top of her mug. "So someone ripped out its pages. Can it talk?"

I smirked. Glanced right and left to make sure no one was in the bakery and tugged it out of my shoulder bag, which I also liked to refer to as the bottomless pit.

"Hey, Reggie. How are you?"

The tome cleared that buttery voice. "The rain in Spain stays mainly in the plain."

Sera paused. "What was that?"

"The rain in Spain stays mainly in the plain."

"You don't say," she said.

I closed Reggie and put it away. "That's all he says now."

"Have you reported this problem to someone?"

"Who? He wasn't supposed to leave Milly's house. I asked her, but she said we'd get in more trouble by telling them what happened."

Sera dipped her finger in the cream and popped the dollop in her mouth. "At some point people will need to find it."

"Yeah," I grumbled. "I'm going to be in hot water over this, I know. Just something else I might get away with that Dewy Dewberry will flip out about."

She leaned back and crossed her arms. "So let me get this straight. We've got a dead double agent, a balding stone that tries to kill you if it's unlocked the wrong way, a Registry with its pages stolen and a seductress for your boyfriend's new partner."

I clasped my hands over one knee. "You forgot one thing."

"What's that?"

"A sister with a compulsion for baking." I glanced around the bakery at the cakes stacked three high in boxes ready to be sold.

She shrugged. "Just getting ahead."

I narrowed my eyes. "Stop worrying so much."

She threaded her fingers through her short, dark hair. Dazzling blue eyes peeked out from beneath a curtain of bangs. "Oh, okay. We've only been attacked twice and almost thrown in witch jail. It's very stressful. This whole Norwood thing has been more trouble than it's worth."

"I know," I said. "I want our family to be safe, not to be worried that someone's going to kill us in our sleep."

She frowned. "I thought Roman had been posting someone outside our house?"

I sighed. "He has. I've seen Steve Howie's patrol car a couple of times. I think he's been more interested in shooting his ray gun at cars as they pass, looking for folks to ticket, more than he's guarding us. But anyway, that's why we have to figure out how to crack open this balding stone. I need Dewy Dewberry out of my life, too, you know."

"Roman said nothing was going on between them."

I sighed. "He did, but I still don't want her to be his partner. She can't be trusted."

Sera folded her hands on the counter. "Okay, so what do we do now?"

I shook my head. "I don't have any leads."

"Does Roman?"

"Not as far as I know."

Sera drummed her fingers on the counter. "You need an expert on balding stones."

"Roman's dad is an expert in the device that unlocks them."

"But that's not the same. You need to undo the magic surrounding it."

I rolled my eyes. "Thanks, Sherlock. Any ideas on how I can get that done since I don't know anything about Norwood?"

Sera paused. "Yep. You go back to Alias. Find out what he

knows. He's got more info to spill. You need to make him do it."

I smirked. "And how am I going to get him to do that?"

Sera smiled. "Take Grandma. She'll get him to talk."

"Why? Why would he talk more with her around?"

A sparkle gleamed in Sera's eyes. "Because he used to be her boyfriend."

***

The next day Roman drove the three of us to Alias's house. Alias invited us down to dinner once he knew I was bringing Grandma along. She wore her best tiara and had been sure to fluff her hair so it was nearly horizontal all the way across the back. She'd used so much hairspray I was afraid to strike a match anywhere near her.

"Are you excited, Grandma?" I asked.

"I don't know what I should be excited about. I haven't seen the man in fifty years." Pause. "I hope he makes beef Wellington. That would make me excited."

I flashed Roman a look. His lips curled into a smile. He thought this was just as good as I did. I rubbed my hands together. Grandma and her ex-boyfriend. I wanted to know all about this.

Roman guided the SUV onto a smooth driveway. Alias's house didn't look anything like I expected. Based on his lab, I expected trees and shrubs to be growing from inside out. Basically I expected it to be the sort of place that would make me itch from looking at it. You know, give me the heebie-jeebies.

Luckily it looked normal. It was cottage-sized with warm yellow lights emanating from inside. White lights winked on the bushes.

"So he keeps his Christmas lights up all year round," I mused.

"Those aren't Christmas lights," Grandma said. "Those are anytime lights."

Right. 'Cause that's a thing.

Grandma fluffed her hair one last time, and we exited the SUV. Roman knocked on the door. Alias answered. He wore a pressed gold shirt, red suspenders and black slacks. Grandma's eyes flickered open a little wider when she saw him.

"Ulysses," she said.

"Hazel," he cooed. Alias floated forward and took Grandma by the hands. They disappeared inside, leaving me and Roman all alone.

Roman smiled. "Shall we?"

"I suppose we shall."

Alias offered us wine. Roman and I declined, but Grandma accepted. She and Alias took their glasses to the living room, where a crackling fire burned in a well-used hearth. They sat practically nose to nose in two wingback chairs.

I quirked a brow to Roman. "Feel like a third and fourth wheel?"

He nodded. "Yeah. Let's go look around."

I balked. "We can't just do that."

Roman shot me a devilish grin. "We can't? Doesn't look like there's anyone to stop us."

"How about you go look and I'll stay here?"

He pecked my cheek. "Your loss. I bet there's lots of dark rooms in this house."

My girlie parts tingled. "You just go on and look. I'll stay right here."

Five minutes later he returned. "Did you find anything?"

He shook his head. "Only a tiny snake that threatened to bite me."

"Sounds terrifying."

He raked his fingers through his beach-blond hair. "If you only knew."

After what seemed like an hour of the geriatric social club, Alias offered us some supper. Beef Wellington, it turned out.

Alias wore a sloppy smile as he doled out individual beef-filled puff pastries. "So, do I understand you wanted to discuss Norwood more in depth?"

I nodded. "If you have more to tell. We're at a loss. We have his balding stone and know that he was interested in transmutation, but we don't know any more than that."

Roman sliced into his meal. "Whatever you can tell us will help. The trail's cold."

Alias tucked a linen napkin into his shirt. "More wine?" he asked Grandma.

She shook her head. "No, I believe this grape is ripe."

That was an interesting way to put it.

Alias chewed his food for a minute. "Norwood became interested in transmutation about a year ago. I knew he was involved in covert operations, but I didn't understand to what extent. He came to me from time to time to ask my opinion about things, but his interest in transmutation was different."

"How?" Roman asked.

"It was special. He borrowed every book I had on the subject. We'd even debate the best animals to turn into."

"Oh?" I said.

Alias nodded. "There are theories that some animals are better than others. Easier to shift your mind into theirs. Rats can be good. Cats, of course. Not dogs. They like to please, but don't do well when it comes to someone pushing their consciousness out."

"So you would debate this," Roman said.

Alias sliced into an asparagus. "Yes. Hour-long debates. I also taught him the incantations, the way to work the magic. He knew them front and back. Back to front." He flashed Grandma a grin. "I'd even go so far as to say he knew them side to side."

Grandma giggled. She actually giggled like a schoolgirl, y'all. It was kinda cute in a weird way. I mean, who sees their grandma get a boyfriend? Heck, she hadn't even been out of her frozen state for an entire year and she was practically dating Professor Crazy Hair. He was nice, though. I had to say. It was definitely better than her dating some jerk.

But I digress.

Roman twirled his fork. "Was there a particular creature he liked the most?"

Alias held a forkful of food out for my grandmother to sample. "Try a radish?"

"Yes, thank you," she said sweetly. She took the bite. "Delicious."

Roman rolled his eyes. "Any animal he talked about the most?"

"Hmm?" Alias said, tearing his eyes from Grandma. "Animals he liked the most?"

"Yes, was there one he told you that he would transmute into?"

"Hmm. Now let me see." Alias chewed a hunk of beef for nearly a minute before swallowing. "Yes, I do believe there may have been one."

"What was it?" I asked.

"Of course, you realize this doesn't mean anything," Alias said. "Just because he liked a particular creature doesn't mean you need to run all over the place looking for one and trying to see if it's Norwood."

I frowned. "Of course not. We're only looking for clues. We need something to help us figure out who killed him. We don't have anything to go on."

Alias swiped the linen napkin over his mouth. "It's just that sometimes people can go a little batty trying to find out if someone has transmuted. Usually loved ones. They think Daddy has turned into their pet cat, and they become obsessed. Convinced puss-puss is their dearly departed grandmother, they do everything to get the soul of the person to show itself, and end up harming the animal in the process."

"We're not going to hurt any animals," I said.

"That's good, because if Norwood has taken the body of an animal, he'll be asleep for a while. They all are. Transmutation takes a lot out of a person. In order to communicate with the being inside the animal, sometimes the animal body needs to undergo a shock."

"What sort of shock?" I asked.

"It can be as dramatic as a near-death experience. Not always, but sometimes. Something strong enough to force the consciousness of the deceased into the forefront of the animal mind."

"So that's what people do to their pets? Try to scare them to death?" I said.

"Exactly," Alias replied.

"Okay, so with all that in mind, is there still one animal Norwood told you he would take?" Roman asked.

"Well, in fact there was," Alias said.

Roman nodded. "And that was?"

Alias smiled. "A snake."

EIGHTEEN

It was late by the time we finished dinner, so Alias invited us to spend the night. His house was small. Grandma got one guest bedroom and I got another.

That meant Roman got the pull-out couch.

I hadn't really had a chance to talk to Roman since all that stupid Dewy stuff had gone on. I'd hoped to get the chance that night, but it didn't look like it was going to happen.

A soft knock came from the door. I opened it to find a shirtless, shoeless Roman. My mouth dried at the sight of his chain-saw sculpted abs and arms.

"Need a blanket?" I said.

"I was hoping for a good-night kiss," he said in a husky voice.

I quirked a brow. "Dressed like that?"

He nodded. "You might need a foot massage, too. I want to be comfortable."

He took two steps forward, swept me into his arms and kissed me. I relaxed into him, let his fingers slide through my hair, felt release as his lips grazed over my jaw and down my neck.

I giggled. "That was quite the good-night kiss."

"It could become a good-morning kiss," he whispered.

He walked us back to the bed and settled me down on it. We stretched out, and he proceeded to nuzzle below my ear. I shivered.

"You shouldn't be here."

"Are the police going to arrest me?" he asked.

"They might," I teased.

He stopped kissing me. Roman's hot breath fogged my brain. "The way I see it, we have some making up to do."

I shrank back. "I think we just did it."

His gaze trailed the line of my throat. "We're not done. You need convincing that you're the only woman in my life, and I need convincing that you believe it."

I sighed. "I do believe it."

Roman slid his hand under my shirt. My stomach quivered. I automatically pulled away.

He kissed my forehead. "You sure about that?"

"How about I'm working on it."

He sighed and rolled off, leaning on his side. He propped a hand under his head. "At some point this relationship is either going to move forward or it won't."

I gave him a big grin with lots of teeth. "I think it's been moving forward."

"It has on my end."

"And that means?"

He glanced at some dirt or something under his fingernails. "If it were up to you, we'd stay right here for eternity."

"On this bed?"

He flashed me a dark look. Roman took my hand and pulled me to him. His fingers traced my cheek. "I want you to get comfortable with me. With the idea of me touching you. If it were up to you, Dylan Apel, we'd never go any further than this. Ever. At some point you've got to let whatever barrier stands between us disappear. Not for my sake but yours."

"How do you know there's anything between us?"

He chuckled. "You're kidding, right? Darlin', I've been studying human behavior all my life. I know when someone's got an issue. You, my dear, have an issue. You hide behind this curtain, ready to blame me for your problem. That's where this whole insecurity with Dewy comes from. But really, it's coming from you. I don't care about Dewy. I care about you." He tapped two fingers to my heart. "Whatever lies in here is stopping you. Don't let it come between us."

I leaned back. "I thought you said you were patient."

"There's a difference between patience and stupidity. I'd be stupid if I let you hide behind your fear. Relationships are supposed to make you a better person. I'm being a better person by making you confront your fear. It doesn't mean you have to jump into bed with me. I'm only trying to have some progress."

"And that progress doesn't mean you want to seduce me?"

Roman's sea-green eyes sparkled. "Oh, I want to seduce you. You don't even know how fierce, darlin'." He wrapped me up in a hug. "But I want you to be comfortable in your own skin first." He stroked my back. "At some point you're going to come out of this shell. I'm going to be ready for you when you do. In the meantime…"

"In the meantime you're happy to sleep on the couch?" I squeaked.

"As you wish." He rolled off the bed and hovered above me. Roman leaned down, his hair tickling my cheeks. He kissed the top of my head. "Good night. See you in the morning."

"Good night." I sat up. "Roman?"

He turned around quickly, as if I was about to invite him back in. I grabbed a pillow and hugged it to me. "You can stay in here if you want. You don't have to sleep on the couch."

His eye twitched. "Not tonight. You've got some things to think about it." He turned.

"Roman?"

He stopped, kept his back to me. The outline of his muscles sent a zinger of desire down to my core. Dear Lord, it was like looking at Thor himself. I nearly toppled off the bed to the floor.

"Yes?"

"What are we going to do next? I mean, now that you know Norwood liked snakes?"

With his back to me he said, "We're going to find him."

"How? We don't even know where to start."

"I know where to start."

"Where?" I said.

Roman opened the door. As he crossed the threshold, he said, "Milly's house."

***

Grandma seriously did not want to leave Alias. I'd never, and I mean never, seen her so kooky in all my life.

And that's saying a lot.

"Alias, you'll have to come visit in the spring when the cherry blossom trees are in full bloom."

Alias had a sappy smile plastered over his face. He took my grandmother's hand and gently patted it. "Of course, I would love nothing more. And perhaps we can have dinner again?"

"Nan can cook, but she's never tried anything as extravagant as what you make. Your Wellington was delicious."

He touched his nose to hers. "There's more where that came from."

She giggled.

I choked on either a laugh or some vomit edging up my throat. Not sure which.

Roman shrugged on his black duster. "Everybody ready?"

I nodded. "I hope so. Any more time here and I'll turn into a pile of sappy dialogue."

He slid on his glasses. "We don't want that to happen." He wrapped a hand around my waist and planted a kiss on my forehead.

We thanked Alias for his hospitality and left, rolling into Silver Springs hours later. After dropping Grandma off at the house, we headed over to Milly's. It was Sunday, Perfect Fit was closed, so I was free to do whatever I wanted.

"You sure you want to come?" Roman asked.

"Of course. Didn't you know? I solve mysteries in my spare time."

He chuckled. "So you do. You're pretty darn good at it, too." He slid his glasses off his face and flashed me one of those looks that made my stomach do cartwheels.

I cleared my throat. "So on to Milly's."

"On we go."

We arrived five minutes later.

Milly scowled at us. "What's got you two looking so perky today? A quickie?"

My hair nearly stood on end. "What?"

"Never mind. Come in."

Roman strode in and walked straight over to the aquarium that held the snake. "Where did this come from?"

Milly shrugged. "Just showed up wanting a place to live."

I nibbled the end of my finger and spat out a bit of hangnail.

"Did it tell you that?"

"Didn't have to. It was obvious. Anyone want some tea?"

I raised my hand. "Please."

She magicked up a fresh glass for me. Sugary-sweet liquid spilled over my tongue and glided down my throat. Delicious.

"So who is it?" Roman asked.

Milly took a long draught from her glass and smacked her lips. "How should I know? It doesn't talk."

I did 'a double take. "You mean you know that it's a familiar?"

She caned over to her recliner. "Of course. Why else would it just appear looking for a home?"

"And you didn't tell anyone?"

Milly tipped her head from side to side. "Excuse me but even a witch in preschool would know what that thing is. It's obvious."

"It's not to me."

"Well, you're not in preschool," she snapped.

Roman scrubbed a hand over his face. "We need to know if it's Norwood."

"So what are you going to do? Take a match to its belly?" Milly said.

Roman paused. He looked around the room. He spotted Polly and opened his cage. "No. I'm going to let these two fight it out."

"Isn't that animal cruelty?" I said.

He wrapped his hands around Polly. "The bird's made of wood. And I'm not going to let anything happen to the snake. We need him healthy, remember?"

Milly crossed her arms. "Those two are friends now. It's not going to work."

Roman smiled. "It'll work if you help me."

Milly smirked. "All right. What do you want Polly to do?"

Roman told Milly. Milly instructed Polly. Polly Parrot flew from his cage and dive-bombed the snake. Polly didn't actually touch the snake, he came just a hair's breadth away from it. He flew back up to his cage and swooped down again.

The snake opened one eye, then the other. It saw Polly fluttering down, watched for a moment and then went back to closing its eyes.

"It's not working," I said.

"You got that right, toots," Milly agreed.

"Any other ideas?" I asked Roman.

He scratched his head. "Nothing that doesn't involve PETA having me arrested."

"We don't even know if it's Norwood," I said. "It could be anybody."

Roman rested his chin in his palm. After several seconds, he snapped his fingers. He dug the marble from his pocket. "This might perk him up."

Roman waved it in front of the snake's face. The snake once again opened one eye. Then it opened the other. It raised its head, its body slowly uncoiling. Its tongue flickered toward the marble.

Its mouth opened.

I blinked. The snake held its mouth open.

"What do you think it wants?" I said.

"I think I'm supposed to put the marble in there," Roman answered.

"In its mouth?"

"Sounds like a plan to me," Milly said. "If this is Norwood, that may be the way to crack the encoding—the snake may have to use its saliva somehow."

I quirked a brow. "Its saliva?"

"You got a better theory, toots?"

I shrugged. "Nope." I glanced at Roman." Well, then, what are you waiting for?"

Roman palmed the marble hesitantly. He looked at me, then Milly, and back to the snake.

"Here goes nothing." He tossed the balding stone into the snake's mouth.

Its jaws snapped shut.

NINETEEN

I watched. I waited. Nothing.

"Um. What's supposed to happen now?" I whispered to Roman.

"Not sure."

"How long should we wait?"

"Don't know."

We stared at the snake for five minutes. Still nothing.

Milly slapped her knees. "Well, looks like he'll have to poop it out for you to get that stone back. I'm not going to sit here that long. I'm going to make some lunch."

"Okay," I said. "I need to get back home. I've got some work to do for the store."

Roman sighed. "I hope I didn't destroy that marble."

I rubbed his shoulder. "It's not like it matters. We couldn't get it to work anyway."

"Good point."

I was on my way out the door, in fact had it opened, when I bumped headfirst into Reid.

"Ouch!" I rubbed the knot forming in my hair. "Watch where you're going."

"Same here," she grumbled.

I noticed she had Reggie. "Why do you have that?"

She blinked a couple of times. "I almost forgot with the brain damage you just gave me."

I scoffed. "Very funny. What is it?"

Reid cleared her throat quite prim and proper and said, "It's talking."

I stepped back. "Seriously?"

She grinned, plumped her burgundy curls and fist pumped the air. "Yeah, and you won't believe what it has to say."

I hauled Reid inside. "Reggie's talking."

"Great," Milly said. "Put it on the table."

Reid laid it down. "Okay, Reggie, tell them what you told me."

The book cleared its throat. "I have been assaulted, Just Dylan."

I nodded. "I know that. I'm sorry. Do you know who did it?"

Reggie gave a heavy sigh. "No. They wore a hood. They yanked out my pages one by one. It was horrible. Terrible!"

I waited while the book had its moment, and then said, "Do you know why they did it?"

Reggie whimpered for a second as if it needed time to pull itself together. Finally it said, "I believe it was to stop me from helping you any more in your investigation."

Roman tapped two fingers on the table. "I'm sorry this happened to you, Reg. I'll do my best to return your pages to you. Thank you for your help. You've been invaluable."

Roman headed for the door. I followed.

The air behind me cracked and fizzled. As I turned around, a gray cloud appeared. A moment later it dissolved, fizzling into swirling cinnamon and crimson curls. Em. Great. Just who I wanted to see. The one witch who never, and I mean ever, made my life easier.

"Roman, I've been lookin' all over for you."

Roman nodded. "You've found me."

Em's green eyes slewed across the room. "Is this all the people who are here? There's no one else?"

"This is it," Roman said. "What's going on?"

Em bit her bottom lip. Oh crap. Whatever she had to say, it was bad. My heart fluttered up into my throat.

She rubbed her forehead. "It's your father, Roman. He's missing."

***

I accompanied Roman to Castle Witch. Milly wanted to pick Reggie's brain, and Reid asked if she could go to Perfect Fit and do some cleaning to make extra money. Who was I to say no to that?

We found Em inside the castle. "What happened?" Roman said.

Em smiled when she saw us, but it quickly faded. "I went to see Boo about an hour ago. He didn't answer, so I let myself in, to make sure everythin' was okay." A sob got caught in her throat. "Roman, the place was a mess. Things were destroyed. Like a bulldozer had come in. I called my guards, had them search the grounds, the castle—everywhere—but we cain't find him."

Em lowered her face. When she glanced back up, tears bubbled in her eyes. She clutched his arm. "Roman, I cain't apologize enough for this."

"It's okay," he said. "I may know where he is."

Em stumbled back. "You do?"

He sighed. "Maybe." Roman looked at me. He started to

walk off.

"Do you want me to come?" I asked.

He stopped. Roman squared his shoulders and looked at the ground. When he spoke, his voice was tender. "I need you to."

A shiver zinged down my spine. I nodded to Em and crossed to Roman. "Let's go."

We strode up the staircase, down one winding hall and up another set of stairs until we reached a long wall. Roman stopped, raised his hand as if to knock. He paused.

He tipped his head down toward me. "Behind this lies a wing of the castle that was closed off years ago."

I arched a brow. "What?"

His jaw twitched. "It's where my mother and sisters were murdered. I have access to it, and so does my father."

"How likely is it that he's here?"

He shrugged. "It's not. But it's better than the alternative."

I swallowed. He was right. Boo being kidnapped was worse than him ghosting the halls where his family was murdered.

"Okay. Fingers crossed," I said.

Roman raised a hand and faced it palm down to the wall. He ran it over a portion of the plaster until he reached what I could only assume was the right spot. Then he made a fist and knocked.

The wall that was plaster and stone vanished. It didn't shimmer. It didn't fade. It simply disappeared as quickly and easily as I breathed.

Another chamber greeted us. It was similar to a foyer, and painted in pink roses and winding vines. A hallway opened up behind it. One side held a wall of windows that tattooed the floor with light, while doors lined the other side.

"Would he be in one of the rooms?" I asked.

Roman nodded. He led me past the room to the third door

on the right. He stopped. I placed what I hoped was a reassuring hand on his arm and gave a gentle squeeze. He flashed me a grim smile, turned the knob and opened the door.

A dark cherry four-poster bed graced the room, as well as a makeup table with mirror, a wardrobe and other basic bedroom furnishings. Dim light peeked through the drawn curtains. At first I didn't see the shadow on the bed as anything more than a trick of illumination. But it wasn't a trick. It was a man.

Boo sat hunched on the mattress, his hands to his face, his shoulders slouched. I stayed back and let Roman cross to him. He laid a hand on his father's shoulder. Boo didn't react. He didn't seem surprised that Roman was there. He simply covered his son's hand with his own and said, "Sometimes the pain is too much. It gets to me."

"It gets to me, too," Roman said.

I retreated back into the foyer to give them privacy. I glanced around and noticed a tapestry covering a wall. My gaze scrolled over the colored wool. An orb in one of the images caught my eye. It was small, resembling a marble. A man held the stone. In the next image, he put it in his mouth. In the final image, the man saw the pictures of whatever the stone held.

I staggered back just as Roman led his father from the room. Boo placed his cowboy hat on his head and said, "I apologize for worrying you and my son."

I smiled widely. "You're no worry, Boo. We're just glad you're okay."

Boo pulled a handkerchief from his back pocket and wiped his nose. "I suppose so. I'll be all right." He tucked the fabric back in place and said, "Now, I know the both of you have better things to do than spend time fooling with me."

We walked slowly back to the cottage. Roman helped Boo clean up while I busied myself with the small village shops and talking to the people. Roman found me an hour or so later, and we walked back toward the castle.

"How's your father?"

He raked his fingers through his hair. "He's okay."

"He about destroyed the cottage."

"He lost it, apparently. Said the weight of everything crashed down on him all at once. He broke some stuff and then went to find the old section of the castle."

I nodded. "Is he okay now?"

"He's better, but I don't think he'll ever be okay."

I sighed. "I'm sorry, Roman."

He pulled his glasses from his duster pocket and slid them over his green eyes. "That's how these things go, darlin'," he said. "You gotta take it one day at a time."

I paused, unsure how to bring up what I'd discovered on the tapestry, until I realized I just needed to go ahead and say it.

"It's not a balding stone."

Roman tipped his head toward me. "What?"

"Norwood's marble. It's not a balding stone. At least, not one that needs the balding device."

"I'm not following."

"I saw a tapestry up in the castle with a picture of a man holding a stone that looked exactly like Norwood's. The man didn't use a device to read it, however. Instead he placed the stone in his mouth."

"Like the snake did," Roman said, realization seeming to hit him.

"Exactly. I don't know if that snake is Norwood or not, but putting the stone in its mouth is exactly what we should have done. Not the snake." I swallowed. "I hope. I mean, the thing did release toxic gas when we fooled with it magically. Hopefully it won't do that if I put it in my mouth."

"Darlin', you won't be the one putting it in your mouth. I'll be doing that."

We reached the spot outside the castle where we had arrived. Em stood waiting for us. I have no clue how she knew when we'd show up, but she was there and for that, I was grateful.

"I'm so glad you found him," Em said. "If he'd really been missin'—well, I don't know what I'd have done."

"You mean like a kidnapping," I said.

"Yeah. You don't want to see this witch mad," Em joked. But she wasn't really joking. I did not, in fact, want to see Em mad. Dealing with Em in her regular surly state was enough, thank you very much.

"Y'all ready to go back?"

"More than," Roman said darkly.

Sadness spiked in my core. It couldn't have been easy for Roman to rescue his father from the demons of the past. My heart broke for him.

He took my hand, and Em whisked us back to Silver Springs, planting us on my front porch. I glanced around to make sure no one was outside, watching. I didn't need to explain to any regular people why I had appeared out of nowhere.

The smell of baked goodness filtered up my nose. My stomach growled like a tiger on the prowl.

"Something smells good," Roman said.

"Yeah, I'm hungry."

We stepped inside. I gaped at the sight. Boxes of confections—cakes of all flavors, cinnamon rolls, fruit scones, spinach and cheese quiches, apple and blueberry pies, pear and lemon tarts, chocolate chip muffins, cream cheese filled cupcakes—everything and anything you could possibly dream of and imagine filled every nook and cranny in the living room.

Some were on plates, others in boxes, but all in all, my entire house looked like a bakery had exploded from the inside out.

Just when I was hoping Sera was getting this whole baking thing under control.

"Um, what's going on?" I asked hesitantly.

Grandma barged into the living room. She grasped her hair as if she were about to pull it out. "Dylan, thank goodness you're here. Your sister's gone mad."

"So I see," I said.

"It's not a joke. She says she needs to bake enough to feed the world."

I glanced at Roman. He shook his head.

Grandma crossed over and grabbed my elbow. "You have to stop her. She's about to make another batch of cookies! We'll be buried alive!"

I groaned. And just when things were almost getting back to normal.

TWENTY

I tiptoed toward the kitchen, leaving Roman and Grandma behind.

I peeked into the doorway to find my sister orchestrating a symphony of baked goods in different stages of development. To her left, eggs were cracking into a bowl. On her right, a mixer was beating batter into submission. Above her head, finished batter poured itself into cupcake tins.

"You feeding the world's hungry, or what?" I said.

Sera turned to me. "Dylan, isn't it amazing? I never knew I could bake so much so fast."

"Yes, it's certainly something."

Like insane.

"Sera, you've used your magic to bake before. What's going on?"

"Nothing," she said cheerfully. She brushed a strand of hair out of her eyes. "Just getting ahead."

"What happened?"

She motioned to a spoon. It plopped into the bowl of eggs and began stirring. "Oh yeah, well. The bakery's closed today. I needed a way to channel all this extra energy."

I gestured to the stacks of goods crammed into every corner of the room. "You're going to run out of boxes before you run out of dessert."

She laughed uncomfortably. "Ha-ha. Yeah. That's okay. I don't need boxes."

The inanimate objects kept right on animating as Sera smiled at me. It was the quirkiest, wackiest expression I'd ever seen on her face. I mean, Sera always has it together, and when I say it, I mean everything. Yes, she's that sister. The one who has her life, as well as everyone else's, sewn up and glued straight.

That's not actually a saying, but it sounds good.

"Sera, who are you planning on selling all this to?"

Sera's eye twitched. "It's going into my online business."

"You don't have an online business."

"I'm getting one as we speak. Tomorrow morning I'm starting a whole new project." She splayed her hand out to demonstrate. "Sinless Confections Online."

I took a deep breath. I had no idea what to say, how to stop this. The eggs kept right on cracking, the mixer right on whirling, and the oven continued baking. I nibbled the fingers on my right hand, trying to think of a way to talk my sister out of this.

Right as I was thinking I'd have to grab a shovel and start digging my house out from under a sea of cupcakes, the back door squeaked open. Brock Odom, Monkey King, filled the frame. His dark hair hung loose over his shoulders, and his motorcycle jacket was zipped tight against his chest.

"Hey, ladies, what's going on?" He stepped up to Sera, totally ignoring the stacks of cakes threatening to topple over, and planted a kiss on her cheek. She turned and gave him a hug. He steered my sister so her back was to me. He gave me a smile and a wink.

"All this looks delicious. You been baking?" he said in that silky Matthew McConaughey voice of his.

"A little," she said.

Brock released her from his hold and took a bite of a cinnamon roll. "Whew wee! That is one tasty treat. You got plans for all these? 'Cause if you don't, I know a whole army of winged monkey soldiers who'd love to get their hands on them."

Sera's gaze washed over the truckload of food stuffed into the kitchen and said, "Okay. That sounds good."

Brock finished chewing his bite and said, "Great. I'll send someone over a little later to pick them up. Meanwhile, why don't we get this cleaned up and grab a bite to eat?"

A look of panic spread over Sera's face for half an second. Then she glanced at Brock and all the fear and anxiety dissolved, replaced with a sappy love look.

Sera nodded. "Sounds perfect," she said. "I'll go get ready."

As soon as she was gone, Brock's gaze cut to me. "I'll keep an eye on her. It's been tough ever since the attack. I'll get her mind off it."

I gave him a hug in thanks. "You're a lifesaver. I didn't know what to do."

He smiled. "Don't you worry. I'll take care of her."

We walked back into the living room. "I'll send folks to pick this up," he said, eyeing the mountains of confections shoved into the corners.

"Thanks. I love cupcakes, but I don't need to be forced to eat all this," I said.

My gaze slewed to Roman. Oh my gosh! I'd almost forgotten the balding stone or marble or rock or whatever the heck it really was.

"We need to get going," I said.

Roman tossed a smug smile my way. "I was waiting for you to say that."

Since his car was at Milly's, we hopped into mine. Roman's six-two frame was suffocating in my car. It was like trying to stuff a giant teddy bear up a hollowed-out watermelon. I almost choked on the cloud of testosterone billowing off him.

We rumbled out from the carport down to Milly's. My brakes squeaked when we stopped in front of her house. I pushed open the door and raced up the stairs. I had to know what the heck was going on with that marble.

Milly didn't answer when we knocked. "Do you think she'd mind if we let ourselves in?" I asked.

Roman drummed his fingers on his hips. "Seeing as I'm representing the law in this situation, it would probably be better if we didn't. She'll be home soon." He shifted his weight onto his right hip. "We know that marble isn't going anywhere."

"We do?" I said. "Can't be sure about that. Someone might steal the snake, or give it a laxative."

Roman chuckled. "Come on. I'm hungry. Seeing all those cakes gave me an appetite."

"How hungry?"

"Darlin', I'll eat whatever you put in front of me."

I quirked a brow. "Sounds like quite the challenge."

We drove separately downtown to Gus's, home of the deep-fried burger. I peeked a glance at Dewy's shop in time to see Rick leaving. I glanced at my store and saw Reid cleaning the window. She'd seen him, too. Darn it. I'd probably have another crisis to deal with soon.

"I can't stay long," I said. "I need to do some paperwork at the shop. You know, the one I've been neglecting the past few days?"

Roman shrugged. "You need a new assistant."

"I think you're right."

We ordered a couple of burgers, some fries and a milkshake for each of us—strawberry for me, vanilla for Roman—and sat down. After eating, we decided to meet up later at Milly's, when we hoped she'd be home.

I walked into my store.

"Reid?"

Sobs came from the bathroom. Giant, hiccupy-sounding ones. Great. Could this day get any worse? I reminded myself not to ask that question, because inevitably it could. I grabbed a box of tissues and opened the bathroom door.

"You okay?" I handed her a tissue.

She sniffled. "Yes. No." Reid threw up her hands. "I don't know. I just thought I loved him so much!" She sobbed into the Kleenex.

I patted her head. "Rick's a jerk. He doesn't deserve you." I knelt down. "Reid, you're so much better than him. You're a thousand times better than him, and when I say a thousand, I actually mean a million."

Reid laughed bitterly. "Love stinks."

"Yes, it does."

She hiccuped a few times and blew her nose. I gave her some ibuprofen to ward off the headache I knew she'd have later.

"You can go home," I said. "I'll finish up."

"You sure?" she asked.

"I'm sure."

She balled up her fists. "I just want to tell him off. Tell him what a jerk he is."

I hugged my baby sis as she sat on the toilet. "Don't do it. You'll feel worse after you do."

"But I think that'll make things better."

I shook my head. "Trust me, it won't. It'll only push Rick

195

away more. Just leave it alone and try to forget about it. Now go on home. There's lots of cupcakes there to eat."

Her eyes brightened. "Seriously?"

I nodded. "Every kind you could wish for. If you get there before Brock's monkey army, that is."

"I'll get fat," she whined.

I squeezed her shoulders and said, "Then your next boyfriend will love you exactly the way you are."

Reid sniffled a little, blew her nose and pressed the heels of her hands into her eyes. "I think I need chocolate."

I smiled. "Go home. A chocolate kingdom awaits."

My sister gave me a swift hug, shouldered her bag and left. I sighed as I watched her go. Though her heart throbbed with hurt from Rick dumping her, it would heal. She would find someone else. That was the easy part. The hard part was convincing yourself to shed your doubts and fears.

I finished cleaning and spent a few hours on paperwork. Bending over my desk had put a kink in my back, so I rose and stretched, taking the opportunity to get some circulation going back in my legs.

I crossed to the front door and leaned my forehead against the cool glass. My eyes glazed over as I watched Main, not really paying attention to what was going on until I noticed a body barging straight toward me.

I blinked. It wasn't just any body—it was Dewy Dewberry.

I ran my fingers through my hair because for some reason I always felt the need to look my best around her. As if she cared.

I stepped back, tripping over a chair and landing flat on my rump.

Dewy entered.

"Oh my gosh. Are you okay? Do I need to call an ambulance?"

I smacked dirt off my rear end and rose, ignoring the hand she offered.

"No, Dewy. Contrary to popular belief, when I fall I don't break things. I'm not eighty years old."

She tsked. "You're getting close to thirty, and it's not that far from eighty in dog years."

I opened my mouth, but nothing came out. There was no comeback I could make to that except, "Only if you're a dog." Dewy gave me a sad, pathetic smile as if I were a hound dog or something. "What do you need, Dewy? Out looking for a pole to rub your breasts on?"

"Oh, ha-ha. No. Actually, I'm looking for Roman."

I smirked. "He doesn't shop in here."

She rolled her eyes. "I know that. I haven't been able to reach him on his phone, so I thought I'd see if he were here. Mmm hmm."

I shook my head. "He's not. But I'll be seeing him later, so I can give him a message if you'd like."

Dewy clicked her tongue. "I totally don't think you should deliver this. No, I need to tell him face-to-face, or phone to phone."

I shrugged. "Suit yourself. But if it's really so important, I can get a message to him."

Dewy glanced around the store. "Well, okay, but I'm only telling you because you sort of know what's going on already."

"Thanks, I guess."

"I mean, it's not my fault my partner ditched me after we went on that one ride."

"You mean when you showed up together at Norwood's?"

Dewy nodded. "Yeah. I guess he likes working alone. But when I get assigned to someone, I stay assigned to them."

"Good to know you're loyal."

"Oh yes, like a cat."

I picked a piece of lint off the floor and dropped it in a trash can. "Not sure cats are loyal. But anyway, what is it you want me to tell Roman?"

Dewy shrugged. "I'm totally almost one hundred percent sure I know who killed Norwood."

I paused. "Seriously?"

She nodded. "Seriously. It took me all day and I missed my manicure appointment, but I've got this one nailed."

"Well? Who is it?"

She smiled sweetly. "Sorry. I can't tell you. I can only tell Roman."

I debated calling Roman right then and there, but I wasn't convinced Dewy's detective skills were any good. I decided the best thing to do was to tell him when we met up at Milly's. After all, if the marble showed one of us who the killer was, then it would only reinforce whatever Dewy had discovered.

"I'll let him know," I said.

She looked at me as if expecting me to grab my phone and start dialing. "I'll tell him when I see him later. I think he had some top-secret stuff to do today."

"Don't wait too long because I don't want them to get away. Mmm hmm."

"I'll let him know lickety-split. Thanks for stopping by." Dewy frowned, a little crinkle forming between her eyes. She didn't look particularly happy to be leaving, but I didn't want her to stay.

As soon as she disappeared out the door, I picked up my phone and dialed Roman.

"Dewy stopped by. Said she knows who the killer is."

"Yeah, she's been texting me."

I did a fist pump of victory because he hadn't replied to her.

"Don't you want to know?"

"I haven't had time to call her. I'm at Milly's."

"You were supposed to wait for me!"

"Sorry, darlin'. I drove by and saw that she was home. I'm here now with the marble."

I grabbed my purse. "Don't do anything. I'll be there in five."

TWENTY-ONE

"Okay, what's the plan?" I asked Roman and Milly.

Milly glanced at Roman and then back to me. "I'll put the thing in my mouth."

I threw her a concerned look. "What? Why you?"

Milly cleared her throat and spit the contents into a nearby trash can. "Because I'm old, toots. If anyone in this room has nothing to lose, it'd be me."

"I'm sure the stone's not going to kill you."

"Think again," she said, pointing to the aquarium. The snake lay in the bottom, his albino skin the color of paper.

"Is it dead?" I asked.

Roman nodded. "Looks that way. I didn't get a vet over here to check its pulse or anything."

"Is it cold?"

"It's always cold," Milly snapped. "It's a snake."

I held out my hands like I was directing traffic to stop. "Okay. Hold on a minute. Dewy says she knows who killed Norwood. Maybe no one needs to swallow the marble, or even put it in their mouth. Why don't we just ask Dewy about her lead and go from there?"

Roman cocked his head toward me. "Do you really trust her lead?"

"Well, no."

"Do you have a better suggestion?" Roman said.

"No."

Milly clapped her hands together. "It's been too long since I battled for my life, anyway. I'm ready to take things to the next level, as you kids say."

I rolled my eyes. "Yep, we say that all the time, but generally not when it deals with death and dying."

Milly dismissed me with a wave of her hand. "Pah. I'm not going to die. It'd take a lot more than a toxic marble to get rid of me."

I looked at Roman. He shrugged. I argued with Milly for at least an hour, but she wouldn't budge—she wanted to be the sacrificial witch. Finally I gave up.

"Okay, whatever you want to do then," I said.

"Great. Get me a pillow. I'm going to lay back for this."

I grabbed one off the recliner and crossed to the couch. "But you might choke on the marble."

Milly shot me a dark look.

"Listen, I don't want you to choke or die doing this, so why don't you sit up and play nice?"

Milly grumbled something under her breath.

"What was that?"

"I said let's get this over with."

I grinned widely. "That's what I thought. Now where's the marble?"

Roman displayed it between his finger and thumb. "Right here." He handed it to Milly. "Do we need a safe word?"

"Yeah," she snarled. "How about help?"

"Sounds good to me," he said.

Milly stared at the marble for at least half a minute before saying, "Here goes nothing."

She popped it in her mouth and clamped her lips shut. I stared at Milly. She stared back at me. I held my breath, waiting for something, anything to happen. Milly sat, poker-faced, as if she too were waiting for the heavens to open or something.

I gave it a few seconds before saying, "Is that it? Should we give up?"

Milly opened her mouth to say something. It clamped right shut. Purple smoke wafted out of her nose.

"Oh no! Are you okay?"

She nodded but kept her mouth shut.

"Do you think she's okay?" I said to Roman.

"I'll force it out of her mouth if her eyes roll back."

Milly jerked. Her hands splayed out and her eyes rolled up into her head.

"Go for it," I said.

Roman strode to Milly, placed a hand on each side of her face. She pulled away. I couldn't tell if she was doing that on purpose or if the marble was causing her erratic movements. But when her body started shaking and she lifted from the couch as if demon-possessed, I was pretty sure all that was the marble.

I rushed over. "We've got to get it out of her mouth."

Roman placed his hands on her cheeks and squeezed.

"Can you spit it out, Milly?" She stared at me with blank, expressionless eyes. "Spit it out!"

Smoke puffed from her ears like a Bugs Bunny cartoon. I flattened my hands and whacked both of her cheeks. Hard.

The marble flew from her mouth. It soared across the living room and hit Polly's cage. The bird flapped his wings and squawked at us.

"Milly, are you okay?" Blank eyes stared across the room. I shook her. "Milly?"

She shivered and blinked several times. "Whew. What a ride!"

I stepped back. "What?"

She caned herself to her feet. "The stone. Being in Norwood's mind was like riding the Coney Island Roller Coaster. Only much safer and not so rickety."

I shot a worried glance to Roman. "Oookaaay."

She stretched. "I feel twenty years younger."

"That's great," Roman said. "But what did you see in Norwood's mind? Do you know who killed him?"

Milly flashed him a wicked smile. "In fact, I believe I do."

I clenched my fists. "Who was it?"

The door burst open. Sera ran in.

"What's going on?" I said.

Sera shook her head. She started speaking but choked on her words. I immediately forgot all about Norwood. Well, let's be honest, I didn't actually forget, but he wasn't the most important thing on my mind at the moment.

I pinned Sera's shoulders. "What's going on?"

She knuckled tears from her eyes. "I tried calling you, but your phone went to voice mail."

I fished it from my purse. Dead battery. "Yeah, sorry. What's up?"

"It's Reid."

"What is it? What's wrong?"

She bit her bottom lip and looked away. When she glanced up, my sister said, "She's missing."

TWENTY-TWO

Roman drove us back to the house. I was grateful, because I was in no shape to work heavy machinery.

"What happened?" I said to Sera, who sat in the backseat blowing her nose and tossing used tissues onto the floor.

"I called her earlier and asked her to pick up milk."

"We're out of milk?" I said.

Sera threaded her fingers through her hair. "Yeah, I guess I used it all when I was baking."

"Go figure," I mumbled. "Anyway, what happened next?"

"Said she had one other errand to run and would be right home. She never showed up. I called the place where she was supposed to have made the stop—the hardware store downtown—but they said she never came in. So I got worried and called her again." She choked back a fresh wave of tears. "Dylan, I've called her twenty times. It's not like Reid to ignore me for that long. I know you may think I'm overreacting—"

"No, I don't. You're right. It's not like her to ignore so many calls, especially with a brand-new phone. She would've texted you or something. How long has it been since you first talked to her?"

"Since she left your shop."

I frowned. "That was hours ago. She might be eighteen, but she's responsible when it comes to family. She would've contacted you." I chewed on a strand of hair, trying to figure out where Reid could be. Worry knotted my stomach. "Let's go home and think."

My arm fell to the seat rest. Roman squeezed my hand. "We'll find her," he said. "Whatever I can do, I will do."

I nodded weakly. It would be okay. It would all turn out all right.

We reached the house and rushed inside. Grandma sat on the couch, wringing her hands.

"I've tried to contact her with magic," she mumbled, "but nothing's working." She glanced up at us. "Do you think my power's broken?"

I embraced her. "Of course not. It's definitely not broken."

Nan entered, sword in hand. "I'm ready to fight. Show me who to ram this through."

"Okay, Nan. I think we're going to wait on the ramming. We just need figure out who saw her last."

Sera nodded. "I talked to her right after she left. That was when she said she was going to the hardware store."

I nibbled the end of my finger. "And that's the last anyone heard from her?"

Everyone nodded.

Roman squeezed my shoulders. "I'll call the station and round up some bodies to start searching. Meanwhile, I'll hit the shops downtown."

I crossed to him. "Do you want us to come?"

Roman shook his head. "Stay here in case she comes home. I'll have my phone handy, so call me."

I nodded. "Okay."

Roman kissed me on the top of my head and left.

"Okay, anybody got an idea of where she might be?" I said.

Grandma shook her head. "If I knew that, I'd know where she is. Like I said, I can't locate her magically. It makes me think something is blocking me from getting through to her."

Sera snapped her fingers. "I'm going to the bakery, just to make sure she isn't hanging around there."

I swept a stray strand of hair from my face. "Couldn't you just call the shop?"

Sera shrugged. "Do you think she's going to answer the store phone when we're closed?"

"Good point."

Grandma rose. "I'm going with Sera. Nan, you coming?"

Nan stroked her thumb down the edge of the sword blade. "I'd like to try this little darlin' out. Mind if I bring it?"

Grandma shook her head. "Nah. We might find you a worthy opponent to fight. Bring it, too."

I threw Sera my keys. "Here you go."

Everyone left, pretty much abandoning me to the house. I sighed. Well, at least it gave me time to think, to figure out where Reid might be. I plopped down on a chair to do exactly that, but nothing came. I decided a fresh cup of caffeine might help, so I went to the kitchen to make a cup of joe.

Two minutes later the scent of coffee was trickling up my nostrils and I was staring out the back door at the house right next to ours—Rick's.

Could Reid have gone there? She was super upset after she saw him leave Dewy's. Did she confront him? Even if she wasn't there, Rick may know where she had been going. I placed the mug on the counter and headed over.

Wintery yellow grass crunched under my feet as I crossed the yard. I shoved open the chain fence door and climbed the steps to Rick's back deck. I knocked. No answer.

A loud thud came from the front of the house. It sounded as if something had fallen. Rick didn't have any pets that I knew of, so I knocked again. Maybe he was taking a nap or something and had stumbled off the couch. Or onto his head. Rick was not my favorite person, not since he'd been such a douche to Reid.

I knocked harder and heard the thud again.

Okay, my spidey sense was tingling like mad. Something suspicious was up. I had to know what, so I turned the knob.

It was locked. Of course it was. I traipsed around front and knocked, this time hard so that if anyone was even halfway asleep, they couldn't help but hear me.

No one answered. I turned this knob and it was locked, too. I had two choices—walk away or put my hand through the door and unlock it. Option number one left a queasy feeling in my stomach, and option number two wasn't much better. The idea of sticking my hand through a solid surface really didn't sit well with me. I didn't even know if it was possible. Reggie said it was, but it had also taught me the illegal truth serum spell.

I decided to try something else. I imagined seeing the lock on the other side and watching it turn to unlock. I pushed all my focus to the forefront of my brain. Magic coiled in my belly. A second later the lock snicked.

Success!

I turned the knob and pushed Rick's door opened. The sun was setting. Purple and gold washed over the living room walls, casting the lower half in shadow.

"Rick?"

I heard something muffled coming from the corner to my right. I swung my head in that direction.

Sitting with rope binding her wrists and her feet was Reid. A gag had been shoved in her mouth, and her lips were taped closed. I rushed to her.

"Oh my gosh," I said, ripping the tape off her mouth. "Are you okay? Did Rick do this to you?"

She panted. "Hurry. We've got to get out of here before they come back."

Adrenaline surged through my body, making my fingers about as agile as sausages. "Who? Rick? Why would he do this?"

"I'll tell you when we get out of here. Just hurry."

"Okay, but you could tell me now."

Reid rolled her eyes as I freed her hands. "We need to get out of here and call Roman. Hurry, Dylan."

I yanked on the rope around her ankles until it gave. I threw the last of the binds to the floor, hauled my sister to her feet and headed for the door.

It swung open. Rick stood on the other side, an evil grin on his face. "Well, well, well, looks like it's going to be dinner for two instead of one."

I stepped in front of Reid, shielding her. "What do you mean tying up my sister? I'm going to have you arrested, Rick. You're going to jail for—for—whatever it was you were going to do."

Rick laughed. It wasn't a pretty sound. In fact, it was like cat's claws scratching an old-fashioned chalkboard. I grimaced.

"You're not going anywhere," he snarled.

"Yes, we are." I grabbed Reid by the hand and pulled her toward the door.

Dewy Dewberry stepped out behind Rick, blocking my path. "Sorry, but you're totally not going anywhere but back inside. Mmm hmmm."

"What's going on? What are you two doing?"

"That's what I tried to tell you," Reid said.

I whipped my head toward her. "What?" I said.

"They're in on it together. They killed Norwood."

TWENTY-THREE

"Why do you have to say it like that?" Rick whined. "Like we're bad guys or something?"

"Because you are," Reid snapped. "You lied to me. You lied to all of us."

My brain raced. Should I hit them hard with magic? Why shouldn't I? My sister had been tied up, so Rick was obviously serious about this—and apparently dangerous.

And you know I never trusted Dewy.

I lifted my hand, felt the magic swirl inside me.

"Stop her," Rick said. "Cut her off."

Before I could even blink, Dewy zapped my arm with a stream of power. I glanced down and saw my hands encased in some kind of gauzy cuffs. The stuff basically glued my hands together, making them immobile. When I tried to use my power, nothing happened. No rush, no well of ability.

I was magic-less.

They were stupid if they thought that would stop me. I barreled forward. I would smash through the two of them and run to the house. My head hit Rick square in the chest. He wrapped his arms around me. It was like being stuck in a boulder. He squeezed so hard I could barely breathe.

"Now, now. Calm down. You're not going anywhere. In fact, you're going to join your sister back on the floor."

I opened my mouth to scream. Dewy raised a finger, and some sort of magic clamped my mouth shut. Great. I couldn't talk. I couldn't use magic. If I kept making moves, these idiots might even paralyze me. Rick walked me over to my sister and sat me down. He talked as he retied Reid.

"Yep, your sister here walked in on us talking about a few things—namely that we'd killed Norwood."

I shot Rick an incredulous look. He shrugged. "I mean, why not go ahead and explain it? It's not like you're going anywhere. Dewy, are we sealed in?"

She nodded. "Tight as a button." She looked at Reid. "You can scream as much as you want, little girl—it totally won't make a lick of difference now. No one can hear you, and your sister can't talk at all. To be honest, I'm tired of hearing her voice."

Dewy shut the front door. "It's totally so sad that you're going to die, Dylan. I guess that means I'll have your boyfriend all to myself. I'm sure he'll be so overcome with grief that I'll have to help him through it. Mmm hmm. Don't worry. My breasts will totally be there too."

I shot imaginary flaming daggers from my eyes at her. I'm pretty sure she didn't notice. You know, being ditsy and all that.

She sighed. "We had to kill Norwood," Dewy said. "For years he'd been on our side. He'd gone rogue, you see. That's what a little taste of magic stealing can do—it turns even the best agents to the other side." She giggled. "Had been on our side for years, but then something happened. We think it was Richard Bane reappearing after all these years. Norwood snapped, decided he was going to reveal all of us, take us down.

Well, we couldn't have that. I'd been following him, traced him to Silver Springs. I met up with Rick here, who'd been sent in undercover to watch you girls while Hazel was in her frozen state—we like to keep tabs on folks, you see."

Dewy fluffed her hair. "Anyway, we tracked Norwood to town and followed him to the high school gym. He confessed he was waiting for you, Dylan. He knew if he stayed close to you, eventually Roman would show up and Norwood could tell him what happened the night Roman's mother was murdered and everything else he'd discovered while being undercover."

Dewy smacked her lips. "So we killed him."

Rick ticked off the list. "First task, get rid of Norwood. Second task, find Boo Bane and get rid of him."

"Why?" Reid asked.

"Because Bane could do real damage to us. He was there the night Queen Catherine was murdered. He saw what happened. That could be real bad for the master."

"Why didn't you just follow Roman home?" Reid asked.

Dewy rolled her eyes. "He would've known he was being followed, dummy. You totally can't just go around following detectives who are ex-witch police. They're smarter than that." She sighed. "I admit, y'all helped us with some things, like finding Norwood's house."

I shot Reid a confused look.

She smirked. "They tapped my phone and were listening to us. That's why it kept going crazy. That's how come someone showed up to Norwood's house that night, and that's also how they knew we had the Registry."

Rick walked over to the kitchen. I heard the refrigerator door open and shut. He entered the room holding two cans of Coke. He handed one to Dewy.

Dewy growled, "Stupid book. I tried to get my name off the

bad list. I'm not bad anymore. Why's that stuff in there about the unicorn? I served my time. It should be gone."

I quirked a brow. Pretty sure killing Norwood meant she was bad.

Dewy blew a lock of hair from her eyes. "It was so hard to steal from you. Y'all know how to fight."

Reid's face crimsoned. "You're the ones who attacked our home?"

Rick tweaked his eyebrows. "Not me. I don't have any magic."

Reid frowned. "Why didn't you just break in and steal it during the day? You tried to kill us."

Rick yawned. He stretched out on the couch lazily. "That didn't occur to us at the time. Besides, someone's always at your house, Reid. If it's not your grandma, it's that crazy lady, Nan. We couldn't just break in during the day."

"So what were you going to do? Kill us and then steal the book? All so Dewy could feel better about herself?"

He finished sipping his drink. "Pretty much."

"I hate you," she said.

"Ah, don't feel too bad. Eventually Dewy put a glamour on me and I went in as the electrician to steal it. See? No one got hurt."

Boy, were these two terrible at this. How the heck had Dewy managed to be a double agent? She couldn't even find one man in a small town without attacking a houseful of women.

Reid glared at the two of them. "So you found out Norwood was a double agent and killed him. Then you needed to kill Roman's dad because you're afraid he might remember some key piece of evidence from the night his family was murdered? Basically your boss is afraid Richard could lead everything back to him."

Dewy clicked her tongue. "You got it. That's the whole she-bang. That, and delete all that bad stuff about me in the Registry, which I did."

"So you moved into town just to do a little murdering," Reid said.

I tried to talk but nothing came out. I grunted until Dewy lifted her finger, and I felt the binding over my mouth release.

"What?" she snarled.

"Rick, you've lied to my family. You've been on the wrong side this whole time?"

Rick grinned like the devil. "Of course. I was sent in ages ago to keep an eye on y'all—I was supposed to report when you started working your magic. I don't have any magic, but my mom was a witch. Turned out I kinda enjoyed Reid having a crush on me. It made things easier. But then she got all serious and Dewy showed up and well, you know, a guy's got to have his priorities." He lifted his eyebrows at Dewy, who giggled.

I shot Reid a look. "Well at least you know sooner rather than later. He's a jerk."

Reid sighed.

"I knew something was screwy with you, Dewy. I mean, who tries to kill a baby unicorn?"

Dewy crimped her lips shut. Her eyes blazed in my direction. "I paid for my crime! I paid for it and now that those pages in that awful book are gone, no one will ever mention it again. Now I can focus on what's really important—feeling better about myself by seducing men who don't think they're interested in me."

I leaned back against the wall. So that was it. That was Dewy's whole thing about Roman. He didn't want her, so she had to try harder to get him.

"Good luck with that," I said sarcastically.

She turned to me, eyes blazing anger. "I hate you, Dylan Apel. Hate you! You get away with everything. You never get in trouble. Well, all that's about to end. Everything you've ever done that the council let slide is about to catch up with you."

She shook her head. "I paid my dues and worked hard to become a double agent for the stupid witch police. I never would've been able to do it if I didn't have inside help." Dewy placed the Coke on the lip of the coffee table and dusted her hands. "Now all we need to do is kill Richard Bane along with the two of you, and we'll be set."

"Good luck finding him."

Dewy pulled a magnifying glass from her pocket. She flashed me a wicked smile. "I don't need luck because I have you, and you're going to tell me exactly where he is, whether you like it or not."

I pressed my body back against the wall as Rick and Dewy approached. She held the magnifying glass toward my head as Rick pinned me down.

"I'm not going to give it to you," I said, trying to wiggle out of his hold.

Dewy smiled. "Not willingly. But you will give it to me." She combed through my hair for a minute and then smacked her lips. "He's at Castle Witch."

Rick released me. "Great. Let's kill these two and get him."

I glanced at Reid. Her face had turned green.

Uh-oh. Time to talk fast.

TWENTY-FOUR

My mind raced. "You can't kill us."

Rick frowned. "Why not?"

"Because what if Richard isn't at Castle Witch anymore?" I argued. "You'll need me to figure out where he is. I'm Roman's girlfriend. I know his secrets."

Dewy and Rick exchanged glances. "She might totally have a point," Dewy said. "We'll take them along for the ride." She shot me and Reid dark looks. "Any funny business and you're both like deader than dead. Got it?"

"Got it," I said.

"I mean, you're dead anyway. Mmm hmm. But if you act up, you'll get it a lot faster."

"Get what?" I asked. "I mean, I'd like to know how I'm going to die."

Dewy paused. "I don't know, but I'll think of something. It might be a knife or gun or even death by magic."

Okay, so that meant they potentially had a knife, gun and magic to draw from. That did not help me. I was trying to figure out how to somehow gain any advantage I could. Yes, I knew my hands were tied and I was being held captive, but Dewy and

Rick weren't that bright—I might be able to talk my way out of a nasty death.

"Let's go," Dewy said. Rick hauled me and Reid to our feet and cut Reid's leg binds.

Dewy snapped her fingers. Rick's living room dissolved. In a blink we were standing on the outskirts of Castle Witch.

The sun had nearly set. We stood on the lawn for a moment. I had high hopes here, waiting for someone to spot two tied up individuals with two obviously crazy people. Apparently Dewy wasn't as dumb as I thought. She tweaked her nose with a finger, and my binds disappeared.

"You're still tied up," she said. "It's just you can't see the binds."

"Then how do you know they're there," Reid said.

Dewy frowned. "Because I do."

"So you say," she added.

Rick jabbed something into Reid's back. "Don't even think about trying anything. I'll shoot you in a blink."

Tears came to Reid's eyes. "But you used to care for me."

Rick laughed. "Let's go get this over with."

Dewy wiggled her fingers. "Take us to him. One misstep and I'll just take you out magically. So don't mess with us," she said.

A sliver of black magic whirled around her finger. She was powerful, there was no doubt about that. I didn't know if Dewy stole extra magic or if she was just naturally talented. At this point I was pretty sure it didn't matter. I didn't want to risk my sister's life or even my own. Of course, I didn't want Boo to die, either. I needed to think. Stall them. Find a way to keep everyone alive.

We reached Roman's house before I had a chance to come up with a brilliant plan. Dewy traipsed up and knocked.

Boo opened the door. When he saw the four of us, he said,

"So you've come for me."

Dewy smiled. "It was going to be sooner or later."

Boo nodded. "Let me get my hat." Boo grabbed his cowboy hat from the peg by the door. "Leave them here," he said. "It's me you want anyway."

"Nah," Rick said. "We're taking all of you with us. We don't want any witnesses."

Dewy shoved Boo inside. We all crammed into the cottage. She waved her hands and nodded to Rick. "That should wipe anyone's memory if they saw us here."

"Great. You ready?"

Dewy raised her palms. "Readier than ready."

"Where are we going?" I asked.

Her eyes sparkled with delight. "To a little place you may or may not have heard of before."

"And where's that?" I asked.

She shivered with glee. "Fairyland."

Dewy clapped her hands, and we vanished.

The burst of magic had blinded me. I blinked several times, waiting for my eyes to adjust.

"Wow," Reid whispered. "This is Fairyland? Why don't we live here?"

Lush green grass growing over rolling hills, babbling brooks and chirping birds all greeted us. The only thing missing from the place were lollipops sprouting on the trees.

"It's awesome, right?" I said.

"Totes storybook."

"I know. Good thing you're seeing it before you die," I said.

Reid cast me a dark look.

"Sorry," I said. "Trying to make light of the situation. Don't worry, we won't die," I whispered.

"We won't?" she said.

"Probably not," I said. "I'm pretty sure some fairies will show up soon and help us."

"I thought fairies hated humans?" Reid said.

"They do, but I'm hoping they hate magic stealers even more."

"Quiet, you two," Rick said. They directed us into a forest. The sun slowly slipped beyond the hills in Fairyland, giving us more light than we'd had back in Silver Springs and even Castle Witch. Leaves layered the ground, crunching beneath our feet. I prayed the sound was enough that perhaps a unicorn would notice. Maybe even Titus himself would hear and come to our rescue.

I could only hope.

We stepped into a clearing and stopped. I looked around, waiting for someone to do something.

"What are we waiting for? Your master to show up?" I half joked but prayed that it wasn't true.

"Shh," Dewy said. "He's coming."

My heart thundered against my ribs as I waited. Sure enough, I heard the crack of twigs and the crunch of branches as someone or something made its way to us. A hooded figure approached. I bit my lower lip. Reid did the same.

"Uncle," Dewy said.

I quirked a brow. "Uncle?"

"Blood is thicker than water, Dylan. My uncle helped clean up my reputation and get me hired as witch police."

The hooded figure lifted his cowl to reveal Smiley Martin. No big surprise there. So he was the other half of Dewy's magical duo—the one who attacked us at our house and at Norwood's. Not to mention, he was witch police gone bad.

"Are you ready to take your true form, uncle?" Dewy asked.

"I am," he said.

Dewy approached her uncle and kissed him smack on the lips.

Yuck. Kissing your uncle.

Smiley's skin quivered and wavered as a loud hiss erupted from somewhere deep inside his body. He deflated like a balloon. As he shrank, his skin changed color from tan to gray and finally to green. When the transformation was finished, he stood about knee-high and had changed from a man into a—frog?

He glared up at me with yellow eyes. "What are you staring at? Haven't you ever heard of a frog prince?"

"Pretty sure that goes in the opposite direction," I said.

"Yeah," Reid said. "Like you're supposed to turn from a frog into a prince, not the other way around."

He croaked. "Things are different in the witching world."

I glanced at Dewy. "Does that mean you're part frog?"

She scoffed. "He's a mutation, Dylan. No one else in the family is like him."

"Whatever you say," I mumbled.

"I knew you'd come for me sooner or later," Boo said, his voice filled with a resigned sadness. "I'm ready. Do with me what you will."

The frog smirked. "Come on, let's get out of the open. I've got a place all ready for them."

Rick pushed us to follow the frog, which let me tell you was rather slow going. It was like following a distracted hobbit—slow and painful.

I prayed the entire time that Roman would find us, but I didn't see how. We'd left no trace for him to follow. No, the only way I was going to get out of this was by my own hand. Reid didn't have magic, and neither did Boo. It was up to me and me alone to save us.

I had to get out of these magical handcuffs somehow.

"So I just want to know, you were the one who attacked us at Norwood's, right?" I said.

Smiley nodded. "That was me, all right. Heard it on that phone of your sister's we bugged. Tracked you with a little magical GPS. I also helped Dewy attack your house, but you're a strong bunch of witches. Hard to kill."

"Quiet," Dewy said. "We don't need any unicorns hearing us."

We reached a dimly lit cave. Torches hung from wall pegs, the light flickering in the damp, cold hole.

After we entered, Smiley turned around in a slow, disjointed gate. There was a lot of ambling and waddling, which is to be expected from a reptile with haunches for back legs and wimpy little arms.

"Now that we're safely here," he started, "I wanted to congratulate you, Dewy, on a job well done. There's a promotion in this for you. You too, Rick, you've been most helpful. You will be rewarded greatly."

Rick fist pumped the air. "Sweet."

Smiley's yellow eyes leveled on Boo. "Richard Bane, you were hard to find. So difficult. Edgar had done a good job erasing your memory." He glanced at the ground. "Too bad Edgar had to turn on us at the end. It's hard to have friends killed, but you know, you do what you have to. Gotta protect yourself. If he revealed everything, he would've brought us all down."

He puffed at an unlit cigar. "When you resurfaced, Richard, somehow Norwood knew. He must've put some sort of magical alarm on you. That's what did it to him—made him decide to go all good again. He felt some sort of obligation to you. Well, I found out he was going to reveal everything and had him killed."

I frowned. "Why didn't he reveal everything when he visited Boo at the cabin? Or even talk to Roman then?"

Smiley shrugged. "He would have guessed we were tracking him, and not wanting us to find Richard, he wouldn't have stayed long. Probably went looking for Roman after that."

"You know Boo doesn't remember anything, right?" I said. "Not one thing. You don't have to kill him. You don't have to kill any of us. Just wipe our memories and we'll be good to go."

Smiley cocked his head. "Good try, but that's not how it works. Thank you for bringing us Bane. But now time's up for all of you."

Dewy grinned. "Which will it be? Which one of you will die first? Let's play a game and see." She clapped her hands with glee. "Oh, Miss Mary Mack, Mack, Mack. All dressed in black, black, black."

As she spoke each word, she shifted her finger from me to Reid to Boo. As she neared the end of the rhyme, I prayed with all my heart that she wouldn't land on Reid. Not her. Dear all that was good in the world, do not take my baby sister.

"And didn't come back, back, back, till the Fourth of July, ly, ly." With the last 'ly', Dewy's finger stopped on me. I cringed. At least it wasn't Reid. I couldn't stand to watch anything happen to my sister, especially since I couldn't do a darn thing about it.

Dewy smiled at me. "Looks like we're starting with you." She sighed. "Stealing magic is always such messy business." She yanked a blade from her back pocket.

I edged back until my spine hugged the curved wall. "Listen, Dewy, you can just kill me. Seriously. Just do it with magic. You don't need my power."

Her eyes sparkled. "I think I do." She licked her lips. "Your sister totally won't mind watching me take your magic one strip of skin at a time." Her gaze cut to Rick. "Hold her down."

Rick shoved Boo and Reid over toward the frog. Then he pinned my arms behind my back. I watched with horror as Dewy closed in on us. She brought the blade to my throat.

"Where oh where to totally start?"

"Leave my sister alone," Reid whimpered.

"Hush now, little girl. Sit there and be good. This won't take long." Dewy slid the knife along the edge of my jaw. My heart raced and blood pounded my ears. "I like it when they're a little scared. Makes this much more fun."

"I said, leave my sister alone," Reid repeated.

"And what are you going to do about it?" Dewy snapped. "You don't have any magic, kid. Mmm hmm. What are you going to do? Cry?"

"Leave her alone!"

My gaze flickered to Reid. Rage contorted her face. She opened her mouth and let out a banshee-like scream. A gust of wind billowed up from behind her and slammed into Dewy, throwing her against the wall. Rick was lifted up as well. He rose about ten feet and fell to the earth like a sack of potatoes, knocking him out.

Reid turned toward Smiley the frog, whose yellow eyes widened in fear. He retreated back into the cave.

"I didn't do anything. I wasn't going to do anything to you," he whimpered as she stalked toward him.

"You were going to kill us," Reid said.

"No no no. Not me," he said.

Wind whipped Reid's hair into a cloud of curls. A gale ripped past her and picked up Smiley, tossing him out of the cave.

That left just me, Boo and Reid. My mouth had fallen open in shock, but I recovered as quickly as I could.

"Oh my God! You got your powers," I screeched.

Reid panted. She pushed a curl from her eyes and said, "I guess so."

I let the shock of that filter into my body. As much as I wanted to celebrate it, we needed to get out of here before we became frog bait.

"Reid, my hands. Can you undo this?"

She blinked and then turned her gaze to me. "I don't know."

"Try," I said. "Imagine them gone."

She hovered a hand over my wrists. Nothing happened. "I'm trying, but it's not working."

"That's okay. Let's get out of here before they regroup. Boo, are you okay?"

"About as okay as I'm gonna be," he mused.

I nodded. "Let's go."

We raced from the cave, Boo leading the way. We got about three feet out when my head rammed into what felt like a wall.

I rubbed what was surely going to be an egg-sized knot.

"Totally thought you were going somewhere, did you?" Dewy said.

I glanced up. She stood about twenty feet away, her hands raised, a wall of magic separating us.

"That was real smart acting like your youngest sister never had any power. Fool me once, shame on you. Fool me twice, shame on somebody else."

My brain twitched. It seriously bothered me when folks got quotes wrong. "It's fool me twice, shame on me," I corrected.

"Who are you? The phrase police?"

"No, I just wanted to make sure you knew the right words. You'll have a lot of time to think about them in jail," I said.

Dewy cackled. "Sorry, but I'm like totally sure that things aren't going to play out like that. I mean, you're doing some wishful thinking and all, which I totally agree with, but I'm not going to jail. You're still going to die."

She raised her arms. Black swirls of magic covered her hands. We raced left but were still cut off by the black wall. The thing blocked us from running for our lives.

I glanced at Reid. Tears pricked my eyes. "I love you."

She gulped. "I love you, too. I'm sorry I don't know how to control this magic."

"It's okay."

Dewy snarled. "Die," she yelled.

Magic blasted from her hands.

From out of nowhere, a stream of power shredded Dewy's magic, stopping it cold. Dewy's face twisted into a scowl.

"If anyone's going to be doing some dying, it's going to be you, toots."

Milly stood just inside the tree line, hands on hips, lips curved into their perpetual frown. From behind her, a mass of unicorn heads rose up from the hill. Titus, King of the Unicorns, shook out his mane. "The baby stealer has returned."

Dewy stumbled back. "No, no. I paid for my crime!"

Milly sent a blast of power at Dewy. Dewy jumped as magic erupted into the ground. She recovered quickly, raising her hands.

Milly's voiced boomed in the forest. "I suggest you go easy and quick, girlie. Don't make this any harder on yourself than it needs to be."

Dewy snarled. "Never!" She flexed her hands. A bubble of dark magic appeared. Dewy sent it straight for Milly.

With one hand Milly used her magic to push the ball back on Dewy. With the other she shot a line straight through the ball and into Dewy's chest. The moment the magic touched Dewy, a white light exploded.

I shielded my eyes, blinded.

Dead silence followed. A couple of seconds later I opened my eyes and looked around. Where Dewy had been standing was a black smudge.

Milly brought her trigger finger to her mouth and blew it off like smoke from a gun. "That takes care of that."

TWENTY-FIVE

Roman appeared behind Milly and apprehended Rick, but not before Rick swallowed some kind of capsule that scrambled his brain and turned him pretty much into a walking, talking zombie.

Drool dripped down one side of his mouth. "Macaroni and cheese. Cheese and macaroni."

Yep, that was the extent of all sophisticated conversation that was going to come out of Rick. Would it last forever? I didn't know.

But I could hope.

Milly whipped the magical cuffs off me. I bent my wrists, working the kinks out.

Milly checked me over with a glance that looked more evil eye than sympathetic, and then she glanced at Reid.

A smile curled on her lips. "Well, well, well. It looks like someone's gotten their magic."

Reid toed the ground, all embarrassed. "What makes you say that?"

Milly clapped her shoulder. "'Cause you've got the glow. The glow of magic."

Reid frowned. "Is that a thing?"

Milly nodded. "It is with you. Magic's seeping out of your pores, girl. Let's get you home."

I thought about something for a minute. "Milly, Dewy bugged Reid's phone to listen in to what we were doing, and her phone kept catching fire. Do you think it was Reid's own magic interfering with Dewy's?"

Milly tweaked what looked like a hair on her chin. "Could've been. Yep. Probably so. Reid, your magic was trying to protect you somehow."

Reid tugged on her hair. "Well, it protected me all right. Saved our rear ends."

Milly wrapped an arm over my baby sister's shoulders. "Come on. Let's get you home."

My gaze washed over the scene. Titus stood to one side with a few of his kind. I crossed to him.

"Was justice served?" I asked.

His stared at me patiently. "Dewy was evil through and through, and we don't have to worry about her anymore."

He rested his muzzle in my hair and nickered softly. Titus lifted his head. "Why, Dylan Apel, your heart has changed."

I cocked back. "It has?"

The unicorn nodded. "I couldn't tell you what it looked like before, because it was for you to learn about and heal, but I can tell you now."

"Tell me what?"

"Nothing guards it anymore, and the key is ready to be used."

I frowned. "What key?"

"The one to Roman's heart."

Titus and the other unicorns turned and walked away silently, back to their part of Fairyland.

Roman came up and wrapped an arm around my waist. I

snuggled into his side. "How'd you find us?"

"Apparently when Milly put the marble in her mouth, it showed her what Rick and Dewy were going to do."

I glanced at my paternal grandmother. "Seriously? If that was the case, why didn't you tell us what was going to happen before we left?"

Milly shrugged. "It was all kind of hazy."

I smirked. "Hazy, huh?"

"Yeah, more like foggy gray than crystal clear. Trust me, toots, as soon as I knew what was going to happen, we headed here."

"So what is the marble?" I said.

"A stone that lets you see a few shades into the future."

"Cool," Reid said. "Can I use it?"

Milly shook her head. "It's gone. Destroyed after I put it in my mouth and harnessed its power."

"Bummer," she said.

"If it let you see into the future, it still didn't help Norwood," I said.

Milly thumbed her nose. "That's because it isn't knowing our future that helps us to see. It's knowing the past."

I couldn't agree with her more.

***

The next morning my family sat in the living room discussing things.

"So do we think they're going to keep coming after Richard, or is he safe?" I asked.

Milly snorted. "After they realize all that's left of Dewy is a smudge on some leaves, I think they'll back off. At least for a while."

I inhaled deeply. That was some sort of relief, at least. "Great, so we can breathe."

Milly nodded. "We can all breathe. Roman said he was trying to track down Smiley."

Darn Frog Prince, or whatever, had escaped during the commotion.

"Good," I said. "Maybe we can find him and I can have frog's legs for dinner this week."

They all stared at me in horror. "What? Is that cannibalism or something? He tried to get us all killed. I mean, Dewy and Rick were in on this whole thing together. They killed Norwood, and then they set out to kill Richard."

No one said anything. I sipped from the sugary glass of sweet tea in front of me. "So. Do we think Richard's really safe for a while?"

An uncomfortable silence coated the room.

"Or, do we think this is only a short break and we need to be on our guard?"

Grandma pulled a tiara from the drawer of a side buffet. She wiggled it on top of her head. To be honest, the thing looked like a television antenna. I guess it was fitting. Perhaps it helped her to think.

She poked a finger in the air. "I believe that for now we must focus on training the three of you. Reid has her power and can join your lessons. We must be prepared. We don't know who will come. Will it be the troll people? Or more of the froggy princes? Will it even be anyone? We don't know. But we must be ready, and we must protect Richard."

Milly drummed her fingers on the sofa arm. "But for now they'll probably regroup. We'll have some time to relax and think."

I nodded. "So we can all breathe deeply for today?"

"For more than that, I think," Milly said.

"Don't worry," Nan added. "I have my weapons ready. I'm prepared for anything, remember?"

I smiled weakly. "Thank you." I rose. "I've got a few things to take care of. I'll be back later, okay?" I crossed to Reid and ruffled her hair. "Welcome to the club, sis. Now you don't have to take crap from anybody about not having powers."

She fist pumped the air. "I'm so excited. I can't wait to see how my magic manifests. I hope it's something totally original. Like maybe I'll garden or something."

I nodded. "Yeah, maybe that'll be it."

I left the house, which had been cleared of cakes and pies courtesy of Sera's boyfriend, Brock. I walked the five minutes to the older, more exclusive neighborhood that I hadn't visited in ages. I'd driven by a thousand times, but I hadn't walked through it. Today, however, the sun shone brightly and I unbuttoned my coat as sweat creeped down my back.

I reached a house with white columns, black shutters, a circle driveway and large ominous windows.

I rang the bell and waited.

The door opened.

"Hi, Colten," I said.

"Hey, Dylan." He stood in the frame, a smug grin on his face. I seriously wanted to slap it off. "Everything okay?"

Moths the size of softballs fluttered around my stomach. I tightened my core muscles, forcing them at bay.

"Listen, there's something I want to tell you."

He brushed sandy hair from his blue eyes. "Sure. What is it?"

I clenched my fists. It was now or never. I needed to get past this. Get on with my life. I didn't need to give this guy one more bit of power over me. Not that he knew that. But, you know, for the sake of my future or something like that, I needed to say these words.

"Colten, what you did to me in high school was an awful thing."

He rubbed the back of his neck sheepishly. "Yeah, Dylan—"

"I'm not finished." He shut his mouth. Good. "You pretended like I meant something to you, then you used me, stood me up at prom and told everyone how you'd taken my virginity. You broke my heart and never apologized. Not once. Not in all these years. But I'm here to tell you that you were a scumbag. I put all my trust and faith in you, and you squashed it like a bug under your toe."

His gaze cut to the ground. "Yeah, I know. I'm sorry. I was a real jerk in high school."

I crossed my arms. "Yes, you were. I hope you're a better person now."

"I hope so, too."

I stood there, not really sure what else I wanted to say. I thought about it for a second and realized that I'd told him everything that was on my chest.

I felt lighter.

"Good-bye," I said.

"Bye."

I left before he even had a chance to close the door.

The station house was only a few minutes from Colten's, so I kept walking. I was wearing heeled boots, so by the time I reached Roman's work, my feet burned. I was hoping he'd give me a ride back home.

That's what boyfriends were for, right?

I pushed open the door. A blast of warm air washed over me. Oh, it felt good. I shrugged out of my coat.

"Is he in?" I asked the desk sergeant.

"Sure is," he said.

I walked past the bay of cubicle desks and reached the line of offices on the back wall. I tapped on Roman's glass door.

He opened it and glanced down. "Must be something serious for you to visit me at work."

"Can I come in?"

He opened the door wide enough for me to squeeze through. "Be my guest."

He shut the door behind me. When I turned around, he stood with a grim expression on his face.

"How's Boo?"

Roman shrugged. "All right, I guess. He wants to leave. To disappear again. I'm trying to talk him out of it, but I don't know."

I slid my arms around Roman's stone-hard sides and squeezed. "He doesn't want to put anyone else in danger."

Roman caressed my hair and sighed. "If he leaves, I'll just hunt for him. I lost my dad once—I'm not going to lose him again."

I inhaled some courage from Roman's musky scent and said, "Speaking of losing things."

"What?"

"There's something I want to tell you."

Roman stiffened. I knew he was thinking it was something bad. "Relax," I said. "Though you may want to sit down."

I sat across from Roman. His office chair squeaked when he pressed into it.

"You've been way more patient with me than lots of men would have been," I said.

"I'm not lots of men."

I nodded. "I appreciate that. When Dewy and Rick held us captive, so many thoughts flashed through my mind. One of them was losing you."

Roman stretched his legs. I sensed humor welling up in him as if he'd been waiting a long time for this moment and he wanted to savor every second of it.

"I realized I might never get the chance to tell you how I feel and I wanted to, I needed to." I took a breath deep enough to fill a ten-foot well and said, "I love you. I've known it for a while, I just didn't have the courage to say it."

Light sparkled in those sea-green eyes. Roman smiled, the corners of his eyes crinkling. He reached across the desk, took my hand and kissed the palm.

Boy, was that sexy. I shivered.

"Darlin', you've made me about the happiest guy in Silver Springs."

"Not earth?" I countered.

"We'll work on that," he said.

My mouth broke into the brightest, widest grin I think I'd ever had.

EPILOGUE

About three weeks had passed since everything went down with Dewy and Rick. Life had returned to normal.

Of course, now that Reid had powers, not too much was normal.

"Why are you unraveling my old sweaters?" Sera screeched.

"Because I'm running out of yarn." Reid sat on her bed, a red scarf big enough to protect the neck of a T. rex sitting in a lump beside her.

"Then go buy some more," Sera said. "Don't just take my stuff."

Reid rolled her eyes. "Please. You haven't worn that sweater in three years. Isn't that what they say, Dylan? If you haven't worn something in your closet for two years, you're not going to wear it again?"

All eyes turned to me. I slowly backed away. "Oh wow, would you look at the time. I'm late."

"For what?" Sera asked, crossing her arms.

For anything that's not here, I almost said. "For a dinner date with Roman. Oops. He should be here any minute. Reid, why don't we go shopping this weekend for some yarn? I bet we can pick up a whole bunch."

"Yay! Then can I sell my stuff in your shop?"

"Er, uh, maybe." Truth was, her technique wasn't bad. Not at all, but at the rate she was crocheting scarfs—as she hadn't yet mastered anything else—there wouldn't be room for my clothes in my own store. "Anyway, gotta go."

I shouldered my purse and dashed to the living room before either one of them could stop me.

"I suppose Reid is over her broken heart," Grandma said.

"Looks like a little bit of magical crochet can fix just about anything."

Grandma stared at the wall, a whimsical expression on her face. "I remember when I first got my power. All was right in the world."

"Was it?"

She nodded. "Of course having my power meant I could also fold paper into animals, so we went through a lot of paper— newspaper mostly—until my parents got tired of stepping on bits of the crumpled stuff."

"Why haven't you ever made a paper animal for me?"

Grandma sniffed. "I don't know. Seems like you have enough chaos in your life, dear. You don't need a paper animal walking around."

"Sounds interesting," Reggie boomed.

"Oh, I almost forgot." I flipped through the pages, making sure Reggie had been properly fixed. We had found all of him in Dewy's apartment. She'd ripped him out—page by page.

"Looking good, Reg. Milly will be glad to have you back." I scooped the tome up into my arms.

"And I'll be happy to return to my rightful place."

The doorbell rang. "Well, there's my ride. See you later, Grandma. Don't wait up." I kissed the soft flesh of her cheek.

"Have a good time," she said. "Watch out for trolls. They like to come aboveground this time of year."

I waved. "Will do. Don't worry, Roman will protect me. I'm sure he knows all about trolls."

Roman stood on the other side of the door. He winked at me. "Ready?"

"Sure am."

He waved to my grandmother. "I'll return her in one piece."

"I hope it's the piece I like," she said.

Roman's face screwed up into a question. I hooked my arm in his and said, "Don't even ask. Don't do it. You won't be satisfied with the answer."

"Whatever you say."

He opened the car door for me. I slipped onto the buttery seat and waited for him to climb in. When he did, Roman turned to me. His lips hit mine in a kiss that was long and hot. My fingers curled around the neck of his shirt, digging into the fabric, probably wrinkling it. As the kiss progressed, I realized I was most definitely wrinkling it.

I was pretty sure Roman didn't care.

We parted to me panting for air and Roman smiling. He slid a thumb over my cheek.

"So where are we off to?"

"How about Niagara Falls?"

He quirked a brow.

"Okay, what about a steakhouse?"

"Sounds more plausible."

He shifted the SUV into drive as his cell rang. Roman whipped it out of his pocket. "Bane." He listened for a minute or two and then hung up. "Change of plans."

"What is it?" I asked.

"That was Dad."

"Everything okay?"

Roman nodded. "Yeah. He called to tell me that he finally remembered."

I threaded my fingers through the ends of my hair. "Remembered what?"

Roman tipped his face toward me. "Who killed my mom and sisters."

I gulped. "Does he have a name?"

Roman nodded. "That's what we're going to find out. Mind if we grab takeout?"

I clutched my purse and said, "Not one bit."

ABOUT THE AUTHOR

Amy Boyles grew up reading Judy Blume and Christopher Pike. Somehow, the combination of coming of age books and teenage murder mysteries made her want to be a writer. After graduating college at DePauw University, she spent some time living in Chicago, Louisville, and New York before settling back in the South. Now, she spends her time chasing two toddlers while trying to stir up trouble in Silver Springs, Alabama, the fictional town where Dylan Apel and her sisters are trying to master witchcraft, tame their crazy relatives, and juggle their love lives. You can find Amy on Facebook at www.facebook.com/amyboylesauthor or email her at amyboylesauthor@gmail.com. She loves to hear from readers.

Made in the USA
Columbia, SC
22 April 2021